I0531516

Baker's Dozen

13 Science Fiction & Fantasy Stories

Scott W. Baker

Copyright Info

"Leech Run" copyright 2010 by Pill Hill Press for *Zero Gravity: Adventures in Deep Space*, edited by Alva J. Roberts

"Poison Inside the Walls" copyright 2010 by Galaxy Press, LLC for *L. Ron Hubbard Presents Writers of the Future Volume XXVI*, edited by K.D. Wentworth

"Chasers" copyright 2004 by PARSEC Ink for *Triangulation 2004*, edited by Barbara Carlson

"Ten Seconds" copyright 2011 by *Daily Science Fiction*, edited by Jonathan Laden, December 2011

"Glow Baby" copyright 2012

"Faerie Belches" copyright 2008 by Sam's Dot Publishing for *Spaceports & Spidersilk*, edited by Marcie Lynn Tentchoff

"Excuse Me" copyright 2009 by Black Plankton Press for *The Rejected Quarterly*, edited by Daniel Weiss, Winter/Spring 2009

"How Quickly We Forget" copyright 2009 by Every Day Publishing, Ltd. for *Every Day Fiction*, edited by Camille Gooderham Campbell, July 2009

"Secondhand Rush" copyright 2012

"Thinking Out Loud" copyright 2012

"Not Rats" copyright 2011 by Untied Shoelaces of the Mind for *Untied Shoelaces of the Mind 2011 Anthology*, edited by Geoffrey C. Porter

"ZFL" copyright 2011 by Every Day Publishing, Ltd. for *Every Day Fiction*, edited by Camille Gooderham Campbell, November 2011

"Call Me Z" copyright 2012

ISBN: 0615719929
ISBN-13: 978-0615719924

Dedication

This collection is dedicated to Kathy Baker, or as I call her, Mom.
She has supported me from the first word to the last, and not just the
words in this book.
Thanks, Mom.

Contents

Space Opera

Space is just so darn big that it takes a big story to even get noticed out there.

Leech Run

The inhabitants of Galileo Station parted as Titan moved among them. Not one made eye contact, but all gawked furtively. One of Titan's dark eyes glared back down at the throng; the other eye remained hidden behind a curtain of stark white hair. Conspicuous appearance was his curse. What bystander would forget a snow-capped mountain of dark muscle? Memorability was not an asset for someone like him.

One body in the crowd moved toward Titan rather than away. "The passengers is aboard, love," the man said.

"Reif, call me 'love' in public and you'll find yourself very uncomfortable." Titan lowered his voice so it stayed within the wide berth granted by the populace. "How many passengers?"

"Thirty-two, lo — Captain."

Titan shook his head. "Hemingway promised fifty."

"If Hem flew so bad as he scored cargo—"

"Any load of leaches will turn a profit," Titan assured the mechanic. "But small load doesn't mean small risk. I want you sharp."

"As ever, love."

They continued through the bustling station to their ship, a little cargo runner designed for intra-system transport at sub-light speeds. Of course, a mechanic of Reif's skill could make a ship reach speeds its designers never fathomed.

Such deviant engineering demanded a pilot with a select set of skills and dubious moral character. Hemingway possessed both. He was waiting for them beside the ship with his ever-present, boastful grin.

"I said there be takers on Galileo, didn't I?" Hemingway said as his crewmates entered earshot. "I done already told them the rules."

Titan's brow furrowed. "Thirty-two? Don't dislocate anything patting yourself on the back. And there's just one rule on my ship."

Titan brushed past his pilot into the cargo hold. It was a small hold, even for an intra-system runner, but it hadn't always been so. Reif's touch here made for ideal leech transport. The customized hold maintained a six-foot buffer from all electrical systems, enough of a gap that even a class-three leech couldn't siphon a single ampere. Despite his extensive precautions, Titan always felt uneasy with such capricious cargo.

Titan surveyed the passengers perched shoulder to shoulder on the plank benches that were bolted to the hold's bare metal floor. Leeches, every last one of them. They didn't look dangerous. On a ship in deep space, they could be as lethal as any weapon.

Aside from passengers and benches, the hold was barren: no amenities, no restraints, no personal possessions, no plumbing. These thirty-two leeches would spend the next two weeks in this metal tank. No normal human would accept such accommodations. Why should they when a starliner would take them all the way to Kilroth for a couple hundred cred? This kind of travel was for people the liners would never touch. Alpha System law guaranteed anyone foolish enough to transport a leech would spend the rest of his life laboring on a prison planet — one too close to a sun for a proper settlement but too mineral-rich to resist exploiting. Such labor colonies' conditions were enough to make one envy the leeches' sentences; they were simply shot on sight.

Of course Alpha was a big system, difficult to monitor. A captain could make a few thousand cred smuggling a leech between planets. Carrying them all the way to a friendlier system, as Titan did, could net a small fortune. Titan demanded twenty grand a head. Alpha's policies on leech-genocide made the price a bargain.

"There is only one rule on my ship," Titan announced again, this time to his hold full of human contraband, "no one leaves the hold." He walked along the rows wishing one of them would do something stupid, make an example of themselves. None did. "There's just one penalty for breaking that rule." He pulled the Berretta from its holster. "Lead."

Blasters, forcecannons, lasers — a leech could drain these of power, make them useless. A bullet harbored no such weakness.

Titan ran another headcount before closing the huge external door by means of a giant hand crank — no automated functions near the leeches. He had worked up a considerable sweat by the time it was sealed. He then walked past the sheepish passengers to the inner door and pounded three times. Reif opened it from the other side. The door to the ship's interior only opened from the inside, a fact that made Titan's one rule seem somewhat trivial. Titan stepped through the portal and let it fall closed with an ominous clank.

"How'd it happen to them?" Reif asked as he resealed the door.

"How did what happen? Their vibrant personalities?"

"Serious, love. Why these blokes end up leechy? Look at that dame in red. She not made up or nothing, but she's gorgeous. How do a pretty thing like that come feared through the stars?"

Titan looked. There was indeed a woman wrapped in a red parka, more attractive than any of the women whose company he could afford. She was his exact opposite, pale flesh and jet locks, small in every way that he was large, velvet everywhere he was leather. And a leech. Her eyes met his through the thick glass.

Titan turned away. "Why do you always ask stupid questions?"

They were three days out of Galileo and preparing to jump superluminal, always a tense time considering the ridiculous illegality of an intra-system ship breaking the light barrier. Not to mention the discomfort of traveling faster than light with a hold full of energy-siphoning refugees. But all Titan could think about were Reif's damn philosophical musings. Why was anyone the way they were? Why was Titan—

Reif burst onto the bridge. "We gots a problem, Captain."

Titan snapped alert. "Patrol satellite?" They couldn't risk being monitored when they made the jump. "Not a ship."

"Worse, Captain."

"Did you just use the word *captain* twice in a row?" Captain, not love.

"The headcount. I get thirty-one. One of them is bloody missing."

A leech loose on a ship was like an ember loose in a hayfield. Life support, propulsion, heat, navigation, sensors…the loss of any one of them would leave them helpless. The loss of several was instant death. Titan checked the bullets in his pistol. Sixteen, plus two more clips of the same. "Hem, run a full diagnostic."

Hemingway slumped in his chair and crossed his arms. "Diagnostic?

That ain't my job." The pilot had not yet outgrown the bluster from his punk mercenary past. Titan chambered a bullet and Hemingway experienced an instant growth spurt. "Right on it, sir."

Titan's steps were long and deliberate as he and Reif left the bridge. "Which one's missing?"

Reif had fallen behind a few paces. "What you mean which one? You think I know them personally?"

"We have a manifest."

"Yes, love. Three John Does and four Janes. Was going to be a rich haul, them paying fifty percent extra for anonymity and all."

"Thirty percent." Titan paused long enough for Reif to catch up to his glare.

"Right love, thirty percent. Slip of the tongue."

"I'll deal with that slippery tongue later. Right now, let's find our missing leech."

They reached the hold. Titan pressed his face to the window and counted. Thirty-one. Damn. "So is it a John or Jane missing?"

"Jane."

Titan counted again. She wasn't there. "How is it you didn't notice she was missing?"

"Captain?"

"The looker. The red parka. How does that escape you?"

"Forgotten her, honestly."

Titan pinned his mechanic to the wall and pressed the Beretta into his gut. "Have you opened this door, *love*?" If the disdainful emphasis on the last word didn't tell Reif his captain meant business, the exposure of Titan's full face certainly did. Titan always kept his left eye shrouded. Even Reif had never seen it exposed. Titan was very secretive about that part of his face — that part of his past — and at last Reif understood why. Below his captain's left eye was an indelible genetic tag, the tattoo that forever marked the inmates of the galaxy's eternal prison colony, the labor colony the devil himself would not visit: K-Traz. There was no parole from K-Traz, no release, no escape. Yet here on Reif's captain's face was the tattoo that never left that steaming planet's surface. For the first time, Reif began to understand how dangerous his captain truly was. Not by the tattoo, by the gleam in the eye above it.

"I...I tried to talk her into it. She refused. She was there when I locked the door. Swears it."

"When?"

"Last night."

Titan stiffened his grip for an instant before dropping Reif in a gasping heap. "If you've killed us all, your death will be the most painful. Find her."

The eight-hour ship diagnostic reported all systems normal. So far. Internal scans indicated no extra life forms in any of the oxygenized sections of the ship, only the thirty-one in the hold and three crew.

"So, numb-nuts let a leech into the ship. This ship." Hemingway was every bit as eloquent as his namesake.

"That seems the most likely scenario," Titan said.

"So where is that British piece of crap?"

"Is he British? I thought he was Irish. He's running counts on things the computer can't handle. Concrete things."

"Yeah, like his head."

"Captain!" The voice came from the corridor beyond the bridge hatch. All hatches had been switched to manual and the ship was running on minimal energy. The jump to light speed didn't fit that equation and was delayed. Hemingway verified that Reif was alone before opening the hatch. Reif scuttled in. "We gots a problem, love."

"Another one?" Hemingway flailed his arms like he was drowning. "A problem like having an energy-hungry leech running loose on a ship that uses energy to keep us alive?"

"Right that," — Reif was panting — "and we missing a vac."

Titan's jaw clenched. "Come again?"

"A vacuum suit, love. She might be outside the ship."

"Or anyplace not under life support." Titan punched the door. It dented slightly. He leaned his forehead to the wall while the other two bickered.

"Can a leech even use a vac suit?" Hemingway said.

"Can if she be class three. They can turn it off."

"What, turn their energy sucking off? I'm more worried about her turning our ship off, love."

"Now you calling people love?"

"I might as well, seeing you done screwed us all."

"Enough!" Titan's face was still against the wall. "Hemingway, run another scan. Track for anything different from the last one, including fuel consumption. Reif, find anything else she might have taken, then come down to the hold and let me out. I want open communication channels throughout the ship. If anyone goes dark, investigate. Shoot to kill. Any questions?"

"Yeah. Did you say you was going into the hold? Are you sniffling?"

"You have any better ideas?"

The hold door clanged shut behind Titan. He used his pistol to point as he counted. He stopped at seventeen. There were more after that, but seventeen was his Jane Doe, gorgeous as ever and very much present. He suppressed his initial impulse to shoot her where she sat and said, "Where have you been?" The question seemed to lack the assertiveness intended.

"Where have I been all your life? I've heard that one. And I'm not a hooker, so you're wasting your time in here, just like that little Australian."

"Where have you been the past few hours?"

Her eyes lowered for an instant before locking defiantly with Titan's. "Right here. I did get up to use the lovely bucket you provided. It could use emptying, by the way."

Titan pressed the gun to her cheek and she stopped talking. "Who's missing?"

"Would you get that thing out of my face?"

He diverted his aim long enough to plant a round in the wooden bench inches from her thigh. Several leeches yelped, but not her. "Who is missing? You were missing eight hours ago. Now you're here and someone else is gone. Tell me."

"Where the hell would I have gone? You locked us in here. Not that rule number one makes wandering the ship a pleasant option. It's a little cold outside that big door."

Titan ground his teeth. He could smell the lies on her breath. "There's a vac suit missing. Any of you could have gone outside."

"Most of us would suck the power out of that suit the moment it touched our skin. Maybe a few of us could—"

"Could you?"

She blushed. It was an alluring thing for her to do. "I suppose it would waste my breath to say it's none of your business." She glanced at the gun then back to his eye. "All right, yes. Assuming I could get into your ship, steal a suit, get back here, then crank that monstrous door open without killing the rest of them. Not to mention that it would be suicide to go EVA before a lightspeed jump."

Titan counted the room again. Thirty-one. He should have shot her already. She had left the hold, broken the rule. His trigger finger knew what that meant. He walked to the door and pounded, gun trained on her firm bosom.

He didn't want to kill anything so beautiful. Her death would weigh heavily on him. So had others before. So would more to come. Was this one any different?

The door opened.

Titan stepped through, slammed and latched it.

"What you mean you didn't shoot her?" Reif opened his mouth as if probing for more words, but managed only to repeat, "You didn't shoot her?"

"Never question my actions on my ship."

"But...how could you not shoot her?"

"I made a call. I'd do it again. You think you could make that call?"

"No. I'd make the call to shoot the bitch."

Only now, five minutes later, did Titan holster his pistol. "She is alive and will remain so until I change it."

"You the captain, love."

"Captain?" It was Hemingway over the comm.

"Go ahead, Hem."

"I'm rerunning the internal scan. You're going to want to see this, sir."

"Just tell me."

"I'm counting thirty-two in the hold again."

Titan and Reif looked at each other then rushed back to the window. "Your lady in red still there, love. What do we do?"

"She's your lady in red." Titan opened an access panel and reached inside. "I'm done being toyed with."

"Now what you doing?"

"Covering my ass." He reached inside. "You get on the comm and get Hem, I need you down here to open the door. Reif and I are going back in." He entered the hold without waiting for a response.

"Both of us?" The color drained from Reif's face. "Why the goodbye am I going in?"

It required a special set of skills to escape a place that secure, skills with which Titan was well associated. There were few possible explanations for how they were doing it, each less plausible than the last. The time had come to start eliminating impossibilities. A breach in the hold wall seemed the most likely explanation. If anyone could find a structural flaw in that hold, it was Reif; he had designed and built it. Now the mechanic was scouring the walls by hand in search of any gap, seam, or panel the leeches might be manipulating. Titan watched the passengers' eyes as Reif searched, hoping one section or another might inspire the guilty to stir or signal a partner. He watched one passenger more than the rest.

"She seems solid, love," Reif declared as he hammered his fist against the last section of bulkhead. The metal did not ring or echo. "I don't think she give for no one."

"It's a ship, not a hooker. Holes don't just open for paying customers." His massive fist clenched until it vibrated. This was his ship. Who were these leeches to defy him on his own ship? It made him weak to have passengers he could not control, to have any situation beyond his control. He would not accept weakness. What choice had they left him?

"We're going back to Galileo," Titan announced. "We don't go superluminal with unaccounted leeches. We turn around."

A wave of discomfort rippled through his passengers.

"So we get our money back?" It was Jane, the one that should be dead. She should be dead again for saying it. Why didn't he just kill her? Titan's shrouded eye twitched as he glared at her. He walked to the door and pounded. Reif followed.

Hemingway did not open it.

Titan peered through the window. No Hemingway. Perhaps they should have waited for him before entering. Titan pounded again. Again nothing. For ten minutes, nothing.

Hemingway was compromised. Had he been captured? Killed? Or was that pompous pilot behind this whole charade? Not that it mattered now. Titan was locked in his own hold. Even his mechanic had failed to find a way out.

But there was a way…

Titan drew his Beretta and stalked to the bench where Jane Doe sat. He grabbed a handful of hair and wrenched her to her feet. She shrieked. He ignored it. "Tell me how," he said. The pistol was against her throat.

The temperature of the hold seemed to drop in the silence. Jane's trembling gasps echoed off the walls. She drew breaths several times as if about to speak. She didn't.

"We've been here before, sweetheart," Titan said. "I am not renowned for my merciful nature."

She spat in his eye. He repaid her eye with the ceramic butt of his pistol. She collapsed.

"What the hell you thinking?" Reif shouted from beside the locked door. "You going to beat it out of her? You gone daft?"

"We don't know who is controlling the ship, if anyone. I could care less how many beauty pageants she has won, I intend to take back my ship. She is going to tell me how she got out of this hold or she is going to die in it."

Jane pushed herself back to her feet. Her eye was already swollen and turning yellow. "No, I'm not."

"Not going to tell me or not going to die?"

"Neither."

"No?" She had endangered his ship, risked everything he had worked so hard to protect. No matter who or what she might be, he had but one option. "Let's find out."

The blast was deafening in the claustrophobic hold. The air continued to reverberate long after the bullet had fired. The stench of gunpowder scorched the stale air. White smoke wafted from the barrel into Jane's delicate face. But she did not fall. She did not bleed. Not even a flinch.

"Is this the part where I say I told you so?"

Titan brushed his hair aside so he could disbelieve with both eyes. He had shot her through the forehead, he was certain. But there she stood. He pulled the trigger again. This time he watched the bullet pass through her face, out past her luscious hair, ricochet off the wall, and topple the bilge bucket in the corner. It was as if she was a ghost. But the truth was more impossible.

"You're class four," Titan whispered.

The silence was louder than the gunshot.

"But love," Reif said, "there is no class-four leech. One, two, three, that's all there be."

"They exist." Titan was barely breathing. "You've heard the rumors. Leeches escaping shackles and locked cells. Ships boarded and left derelict without a single forced hatch. As much energy as they are human, channeling their whole bodies through conductive material."

Reif trembled. "Thought those was bedtime stories for bad boys and girls."

"How many of you are class four?" Titan said.

There was a flash behind Titan's back followed by a new voice, "Just the two of us." Everyone turned.

The words came from a plain-looking male approaching from the interior hatch despite not having opened it. Blond hair, blue eyes, shabby brown pants and overcoat — five others in the hold could have been his brothers. He blended as readily as his lovely partner stood out. But he was the only one pointing a blaster at Titan.

"About time, you bloody pirate," Jane said in a mockingly grateful voice. "This brute shot me. I could have gotten a powder burn."

"Tragic," the pirate replied with equal sarcasm, his eyes and weapon still locked on Titan. "Now be a doll and conduct yourself through the door. This ship needs a new destination. You'll find no competition on the bridge."

"What took so long if you weren't setting new coordinates?"

"Bathroom break." The pirate's smirk faded. "I grew tired of the lovely bucket. Now go."

She pressed her lips together and approached the door. Her fingertips brushed across the metal surface. Orange sparks hissed from her nails where they touched. Her palm swept back across, trailing a fountain of sparkling blue lightning. She pressed both hands to the steel and a dazzling halo sputtered around and through her fingers. She stepped forward and exploded into a billion fluttering fireflies that spun and danced and sizzled and whined before fading from sight. The light show cleared to reveal Jane smiling back through the hatch's window. She wiggled her fingers in a mocking wave before disappearing in the direction of the bridge.

The pirate smiled. "She definitely has her uses. A bit of a showoff, really. You'd never catch me making such a spectacle out of a simple door. Just zip-zap and I'm through."

Titan's brow quivered behind its white curtain. This guy was a talker. He could make use of that.

"So only the two of you can walk through walls?" Titan scanned the terrified faces on the benches and turned his pistol on the frailest young female. He grabbed her tiny wrist. "So I can shoot you?" The girl shrieked and tried to duck away.

"Be my guest," the pirate said evenly. "You won't sway my favor threatening her."

"No loyalty among leeches?"

"My loyalty is to my cred account."

"So love," Reif interrupted awkwardly, "is you two in this with Hemingway, or he be dead?"

"Your pilot?" the pirate scoffed. "I offered him a million cred if he could bring me an unregistered FTL vessel. Little punk actually expected me to pay."

Titan released his grip on the terrified girl. "So he's dead."

The pirate cocked his head and approached Titan. "You don't seem too torn up over it. No loyalty among smugglers?"

"You're going to kill everyone anyway. No point blubbering over who's first in line."

"Spoken like a true mercenary."

"I wasn't finished." Titan's muscles tensed but he held his place. "A pilot is of little use to me if I'm locked away at gunpoint. Hemingway is far more useful as a martyr."

"A martyr?" The pirate laughed.

"Sounds nicer than sacrificial lamb. His death reveals you as the murderous snake you are. It tells everyone in this hold exactly what you're capable of."

The leeches shuffled uncomfortably for a second time.

"You've bored me now." The pirate pointed the blaster at Titan's throat and squeezed the trigger.

Nothing happened.

The blaster trembled in the pirate's hand. He pressed again. And again. Still nothing.

Titan took four steps forward, all he required to close the gap between them. The barrel of the blaster now rested between his oversized pectorals, bunching the material of his black tank top into the crease at his sternum.

The blaster dropped to the floor with a clatter. "So we're at an impasse," the pirate said, backing away. His entire body was shivering. "Your bullets can't touch me, and one of your passengers seems to have quenched his thirst with my gun. Where do we go from here?"

Titan dropped the clip out of his Beretta and ejected the chambered round. The time for guns had ended. Time to do things the old-fashioned way. He cracked his knuckles.

The pirate watched the massive black fingers pop in sequence, then he turned and scrambled for the door. He didn't make it. Thirty leeches flowed as a single furious entity, blockading his escape. A dozen arms pulled him down. The frail young female Titan had threatened was the first to kick the pirate in the ribs. She was not the last. The mob's violence intensified, scratching and beating and cursing the traitorous pirate leech.

Titan turned his back to the distasteful scene. He stepped into Reif's eye line so the mechanic wouldn't have to watch either. "One down," he said barely loud enough for Reif to hear over the ruckus.

"Fat lot of good it does us in here." Reif leaned to see past Titan's wide torso. He didn't seem to like the view and looked back to Titan's face. The white mane had been pulled behind the massive shoulders, again revealing the tattoo. Reif's eyes lingered there. "How'd you do it? Thought that planet was inescapable."

"It is," Titan said. "Unless you can slip your chains and get through two huge metal doors, find a way to neutralize the guards' stun rods and steal a prisoner transport. Deactivating surveillance helps, too."

"Did all that," Reif said, "and you can't get out of this tin box?"

"Oh, I can get out. I just didn't want to do it this way."

"Which way, love?"

Titan stepped to the door and slid his hand across the surface the same way Jane had minutes before. The same orange and purple lightning crackled from his fingertips. It felt hot, hotter than he remembered. He hadn't conducted since escaping K-Traz. He'd never liked the sensation of it, like breathing hot embers. But he had no choice left. The sparks grew as he pressed his body against the metal. A million white hot razorblades scuttled across his flesh. His breath left him. He stepped through, emerging whole and pain-free in the ship's corridor. He paused long enough to release Reif before sprinting to the bridge.

The bridge door was open when he arrived. Jane was at the helm adjusting coordinates.

Titan stepped into the doorway, filling it. "I never conducted a bullet. Nice trick. Never occurred to me to get shot so I could try."

A callous smile was on her lips when she turned. "Caldor owes me fifty cred. Mind you, I had you pegged at class-three, not four. But I knew you were one of us."

"Caldor? Your big-mouthed associate? You might have a time collecting that bet. I could arrange for you to join him directly."

Her smile wavered but did not vanish. "So it seems I'm in the market for a new partner. Know anyone suitable? The perks of the position are pretty good."

Titan scoffed. "I thought you weren't a prostitute."

"I said I wasn't a hooker. We're all prostitutes."

"Poetic semantics."

"Is that a yes or a no?"

"I should have strangled you when I had the chance."

"So it's a no." She sighed. "I guess this is the part where I drain the power from life support and watch you die."

The laugh Titan emitted was both taunting and incredulous. "Without your vac suit? You don't look much like the suicide type."

"I'm not much on surrender either."

"Fine. Every panel in the ship grants access to the power supply for life support. You can bleed every last joule out of the carbon dioxide filters from where you stand. I can't stop you from here." He took a step toward her. It would take several more before she was in arm's reach, but he stopped with one. No need to panic her yet.

"Are you calling my bluff?"

"Were you bluffing?" He took another step.

She examined Titan from black boots to white locks before saying, "Probably. Corner a wild animal, you never know what she might do."

"I doubt I'd be the first to hope you were that wild. I may well be the last."

"You must have been pretty wild yourself to score such a lovely tattoo. Rape and murder? Or was it tax evasion?" She was trying to appear cool, but nerves were getting the better of her. She was practically panting.

"Piracy," Titan confessed. "I once made a lot of cred doing the same thing you're doing. Until I learned a lesson or two. Five years laboring under that searing white sun helps a man remember his lessons. For instance, never hijack cargo that can fight back — your pal Caldor learned that one today."

"Caldor hasn't learned a thing since he flunked out of grade school. And I doubt you let him live long enough to apply his lesson."

"I never touched him."

She nodded. "Hence the lesson." She was starting to sweat. "And what will my lesson be?"

Titan grinned. "Not to breathe so fast with the CO-two filters are down."

She gasped, another bad idea in the stale air. The last hints of color drained from her face as she surveyed the life support controls behind her. They were dark, all needles pointing to zero. "When did you do that?"

"Long before I shot you."

Jane nodded, then collapsed. Titan caught her. With the filters down, it wouldn't be long before Titan's body gave out as well. Only the energy he had siphoned from the filtration system was keeping him conscious now, like an injection of adrenaline. It had been a long time since he had consumed that much raw energy. He'd forgotten how intoxicating it could be. Still, his body needed air. He laid her less than gingerly on the floor and triggered the comm.

"That suit ready?" The effort of speaking drained Titan faster.

"Just barely got mine on, love. There in a pop. You neutralize the little lady?"

"Just get here." Then Titan passed out.

Titan woke on the floor of the hold. How had he gotten here? Reif certainly wasn't strong enough to drag him this far.

"Two of them helped pull you here," Reif said as if reading his captain's mind. Reif was in a vac suit, helmet removed. "You're too damn big to stuff into one of these suits when you go noodle like that. So it be drag you or leave you to die."

"My head," Titan moaned as he realized how much pain the hypercarbia had left him in. "You sure you made the right choice? Who's flying the ship?"

"Managed to put in for the closest planet all by me onesie. Impressed?"

"Astounded." Titan sat up and rubbed his temples. "Main life support still out?"

Reif nodded. "Smart we set the hold on a separate system, eh love?"

"Smart." Titan had never envisioned things working quite this way, using the hold as a lifeboat after the main system had been leeched. He had always pictured it the other way, cutting the secondary life support to subdue an angry leech mob. But this worked. Now what?

"I'm sorry I never told you," Titan said.

"Told what? That you an energy thirsty mutant with the power to walk through walls and slurp the juice out a whole ship's environmental system? No worries. On the subject, I'm a three-headed dingo and I breathe fire and poop creds. Just thought you should know, less it be handy sometime."

"I knew you'd understand."

"Understand nothing. Like why you didn't know they could get out the hold like they done, seeing you done it escaping K-Traz and all."

Titan pulled the hair over his face. "I…you could call it selective blindness. I heard stories, but I had never encountered another class-four. Not one, and I spent years searching. Now I had two on my own ship?" Titan shook his head. "I almost hoped they were fours, but I didn't believe." He gazed at the floor. "Did she make it?"

Reif inclined his head toward a red bundle tied to one of the benches with polyvinyl cord — very nonconductive. She was unconscious but breathing. "What's in your mind for her, love?"

Titan rubbed the mark beneath his left eye. "Let's drop her off someplace hot. I want to be sure she remembers her lessons."

Poison Inside the Walls

The vein of fungus wound through the sand and rocks like a crimson serpent, deliberate and steady in its climb up the rugged hillside. The swollen bulbs pressed each other for shoulder room, each a ripe boil crowded among hundreds of its brethren.

One by one, the mushrooms' taut flesh wilted, wrinkled, darkened. The edges browned then blackened in seconds. The hemispherical bodies crumpled, turned to ash, and vanished in the wind, leaving nothing behind but a black streak of carbon from the flame that destroyed it.

Ashia watched the row of boils dissolve under the heat of her flamer. She glanced over her shoulder. The rest of the scout squad was busy eradicating their own patches of boils, the closest woman still thirty meters distant. Ashia pulled the center grenade off her belt and unscrewed the false top, revealing the hollow compartment within. She glanced again. Still clear. She snatched a handful of boils off the rock and crammed them into the secret canister. She resumed her torching long enough for a third glance, stuffed another handful, and screwed the lid back in place.

"Ashia!"

Had she been spotted? Ashia snapped the contraband into her belt before replying to the voice in her helmet. "Go ahead." Her voice seemed shaky. She took a breath and turned.

One of the younger soldiers, a girl named Gretchen, ran toward her, still far enough away for Ashia to dispute whatever the girl might have seen. It would be foolish for so green a soldier to challenge the word of an older woman. Ashia stood her ground and awaited the accusation.

"A hole," Gretchen said instead, pointing the way she had come. "I found a hole. You said to report—"

"To the lieutenant, not me." So the girl had not witnessed anything.

Good. But a hole in the ground could mean even bigger problems. "How big is the hole?"

"Large enough for a human."

"Is it large enough for a Kree?" Ashia contemplated the young soldier's vacant stare. "Show me."

The hole was large enough for Ashia to crawl into. Could a Kree work its broad shoulders through it? Not quickly, but perhaps. She called the lieutenant, who agreed. Time to go. The squad was back in the scout pods and mobile within a minute.

A gas team would saturate that hole and an air strike would collapse it before any ground troops returned. There probably weren't any Kree in there, but it would be suicide to go in for confirmation, even with a full battalion. The humans of Tora had learned that the hard way half a century ago.

Ashia's eyes slid between the horizon and the mushroom-covered crags that lined the route back to the city of Echo. Already the patches of red were thinning, replaced by powder gray residue of scorched boils. Gray spaces were safe; no Kree burrow was ever more than a few meters from a crop of their only fare. Each of the five cities on Tora sat inside such a sooty ring, islands burnt into a sea of scarlet.

The squad returned to the high walls to find the city garrison on high alert. Fifteenth Squad had been ambushed by a contingent of five Kree armed with plasma throwers. One pod destroyed, all hands lost. The second pod escaped with five of its six warriors intact, including a wet-behind-the-ears lieutenant who confirmed two Kree killed. It was the first such attack in years.

Ashia debriefed with the rest of her crew and was free from duty within the hour. Their little hole would not be gassed or bombed; it would disappear in the craze over the attack. Several days might be spent in the pursuit of three Kree out of...fifty? fifty thousand? No one knew how many were still on Tora. But in the long run, nothing would change over a single scout pod and seven dead women.

But Ashia could not let that distract her. Instead she focused on the canister of fungus concealed in her pocket. And on Kurtas.

Kurtas was sixteen, of breeding age for a year and yet to plump a single womb. Thank Messiah. But a bull that produced no calves was destined for the slaughterhouse. If Kurtas didn't do a better job pretending, he would be evicted from the rooster house and forced into a trade. What trade could such a fragile boy handle? No, he needed the leisure of a rooster lifestyle to cover for his true vocation.

"You're early," Kurtas said as he closed the door behind Ashia. There was accusation in his voice. "You're never early. Did anyone see you?"

Ashia stepped into the sparsely furnished dormitory. She wrinkled her nose against the stench of chemicals. "I don't want to carry this crud around any longer than I have to." She thrust the canister at him. "Can't you find someone—"

"You know I can't. Not that I can trust." He rubbed his bald scalp. He looked paler than usual, gaunt. His cheekbones threatened to poke through his flesh.

"I won't be any good to you if I get caught," Ashia said. "Even once. We destroy that stuff, we don't—"

"Please, Mother, not again."

Mother? "Do not call me that. If someone heard—"

"In a rooster's crib? Even a Kree couldn't hear through these walls."

"Get yourself out of the habit. You call me Ashia or you call me nothing."

"Whatever alleviates your shame." Kurtas turned his back and walked to the kitchen. No, not a kitchen; it was a lab, a factory. It was where he turned boils into Puff, transformed one poison into another.

He emptied the fungus into a mason jar and returned the empty canister. She palmed it and slid it back into her pocket.

"How are you?" she asked, trying to be the mother he was not allowed to acknowledge. She never was very good at it. "Is it keeping the pain in check?"

Kurtas's shook his head. "Most of the time. I ran out last week."

"Ran out? I brought you a full batch."

Kurtas shrugged.

"You've been selling again." The motherly affectation was gone. "You're a rooster, for Messiah sake. The city supplies everything, what do you need money for?"

"What I do with it is my business."

"I bring them for *you*, not those junkies. You need Puff, fine; I made my peace with that. But don't you endanger this colony—"

"Endanger the colony? AAs if you love these people so much? They'll get their Puff somewhere and you know it."

It was a tired argument. He would say it will happen anyway, she would say the existence of evil doesn't make it okay to be the devil, he would say his life was its own hell, she would apologize. The cycle never broke. They would yell and curse and next week she would bring him another batch of boils.

Ashia felt filthy leaving the rooster house, worse than she ever had leaving a bed there. She needed cleansing. It was the reason she went to the nursery.

There he was. Elias. He was so big compared to the others, as big as the five-month old in the crib next to his despite being seven weeks younger.

The nanny on duty was a stocky man, well-muscled for his station but morbidly unattractive. Ashia had bedded him just after Elias was born. The act improved the man's status. A decorated warrior like Ashia was quite a résumé bullet, almost enough to overcome his genetic shortcomings. Ashia could not remember the diminutive man's name.

"He's had a big day today," the nanny said when he saw her. "He rolled over on his own and held his own bottle. As advanced a child as I've seen. I bet he walks by nine months. We're all proud of him. His father will be proud, too."

Ashia had been smiling at her infant son, but the mention of his father shattered that smile. "What do you think you know of Elias's father?"

"Everyone knows his father." The voice was not the nanny's. It was deeper, melodious, dripping with arrogance. Most women melted at the sound of Hector's voice. Ashia winced.

She turned and beheld him. If ever there was a man devoid of genetic shortcomings, it was Hector. Wavy black hair, perfectly shaped pectorals, legs like a stallion, face carved out of marble. The biologically perfect mate. A conversation with the man revealed his weakness: an overwhelming love for Hector at the expense of all else.

"Rumors are the poison of civilization," Ashia said, not sure whether she was addressing Hector or the nanny. "You shouldn't heed them."

"He is a fine specimen," Hector said of Elias. He was ignoring her words again. Chauvinism should have died with the rest of the males of Tora. Hector was old-fashioned that way.

"Of course he is a fine boy," Ashia said. "He takes after his mother."

"And his father."

He did indeed. A mane of thick curls already covered the infant's scalp. His complexion was darker than the other children's. His eyes, the same almond shape. Any fool could see Hector in the child. Ashia refused to admit it.

Their meeting had been consensual; its finale had not. She had tried to dissuade him, to fight him away. She was weak. Every time she looked at Elias she was reminded of the only time in her life she had been weak. It was a shame she could never confess.

She was a war hero, a survivor of the Second Wave, a slayer of a dozen Kree in her time. Even the songs from the days of male warriors boasted few to compete with Ashia. To sire her first son — first known son — was a great honor, a boon to a male's standing like none other. Ashia could give such a boost to the likes of Hector but could do nothing for her other son, not even claim him.

"Hector, you did not sire Elias." The lie simply leapt from her mouth.

"No?" Hector seemed to be wrestling between anger and amusement. "The frigid one bedded two inside the same month. Unprecedented. Who is this rival stud?"

"My partners are no business of yours." She had not copulated with another man within months of Hector. She hated sex. She partook only when she had something to gain, like the favor of her child's caregiver. It was her patriotic duty to bear children, but she didn't have to enjoy the process.

"The child's lineage is the colony's business" Hector said. "We can't have the boy growing up to mate with a sireling, can we?"

Damn. It was law. Every child's lineage was public domain for just that purpose. Nowadays, paternity meant nothing more than bragging rights to a male. But there was a time when siring a healthy child — especially a male child — was the highest badge of honor a man could wield. After the Day of Genocide, young women grew old waiting for a mate. Now there were as many young men as young women, but elder women still sought their share. The Toran male became nothing more than a walking sperm depository. Without the laws of lineage, Elias's generation would surely inbreed itself into extinction.

Who else might claim her child? There were many men who would leap at the coup in all its falsehood. But paternity was a routine test and Hector was just the type of ass to demand it. Hector would match half of Elias's chromosomes. Could anyone compete with such a claim?

Perhaps one.

"The sire is a young rooster called Kurtas."

"You said what?" Kurtas was usually mellow after a Puff. He must have known something was amiss when his mother suggested he take one. He had complied, but the news shattered any semblance of serenity.

"I don't want the colony believing that bastard is Elias's father."

"That bastard *is* his father. You don't think a test will prove it?"

"Your DNA will match Elias as much as Hector's."

Kurtas threw a nebulizer across the room. It struck the wall with the sound of splintering plastic. "Match as a sibling, not a parent. Half of you flows through me, but not the same half in Elias."

"No," Ashia said calmly. "But it's a funny thing about incest. You have half of my DNA and half your father's…which is half of mine."

"Incest?"

She had never told him. It had been common enough in the early times — after the Day of Genocide — for relatives to procreate out of ignorance or desperation. Bloodlines thinned, sickness ran rampant. Thus the laws of lineage came into being. Children of incest were killed when they became known, murdered in the name of genetics.

Ashia's mother had fallen in love with Tam, a man vile enough to canonize Hector. To keep his favor, she promised him the virginity of her only daughter — his daughter, Ashia. From this union came Kurtas.

Ashia had fled the city of Beta to protect the life of her unclean child. They fell in with a group of refugees from the wilds, survivors of a lost settlement destroyed by the Kree. They entered Echo as one of them. Kurtas was raised among the orphans, told of his mother when he was twelve, told of his father today.

Kurtas grabbed another Puff and drained it. Ashia made no protest.

"There was never a reason to tell you," Ashia said while Kurtas's eyes were still rolled back. She couldn't be sure he heard. "Tam was expelled from the cities as a pedophile when you were six. The odds of you mating a sibling were remote."

Kurtas slumped heavily into a cushion. "Is that where the D-Gen comes from? My thin blood, my vertical family tree, is that why I can't take a breath or a step without the burning? Never a reason?"

Ashia swallowed. "Part of it, I have no doubt. That and my youth. I was twelve, Kurtas. My body was not ready. We have talked—"

"So they will find out." Kurtas rose again, strode toward the kitchen and his stash but returned empty-handed. "When they do the test, they will find my disease, my weakness. I'll be expelled. Or killed." As if there was a difference for him. A warrior might survive outside the walls, but never Kurtas.

"Why would they find the D-Gen? That's not what they're looking for."

"It is genetic, Mother; it will stare them in the face. All this time you claim you're protecting me, and your lie will expose me."

"We don't know that."

Kurtas drew a labored breath through his nose. Then another. He rubbed his sternum. "You patrol tomorrow?"

He had changed the subject. He did that when he was frustrated. "We should resume patrols, yes. There are Kree to be hunted."

"I need another batch."

"I brought you one today."

"I need another. I have an order to fill."

Ashia stood. She was several centimeters taller and moved close the way she did with young officers that crossed her. "Things have changed. There was an attack. We won't be burning fungus and I certainly won't be free to grab any. It will be a few days at least."

"A shame. Perhaps no one will support your claim after all. Maybe I will deny that we mated. Maybe I will tell more truth than that."

"Blackmailed by my own son?"

Kurtas laughed. It was a humorless, malicious sound. "Son or sire? You cannot claim me both, woman."

Woman? It was Ashia that took a step back. "So you are learning the ways of this moon after all." She sighed, defeated. "If that is your game. Tomorrow. And tomorrow you submit for the test."

"In that order." Kurtas nodded.

Ashia's eyes slid between the horizon and the ash-covered crags that lined the route to the site of Fifteenth Squad's ambush. Her scout pod bounded over the Toran terrain, three identical pods lumbering behind, twice the usual contingent. The pair of aircraft overhead was also beyond the norm. Confrontation was expected. Ashia almost hoped for it; a few Kree might just distract her from all the lies.

She surveyed her crewmates and reconsidered her desire for combat.

None of these others had ever seen a real Kree, let alone killed one. The other pods' crews were no more experienced. Three of the women were rookies mere days out of the training academy, replacements for yesterday's deceased. All of them looked terrified.

They passed acres of rock scarred with the powder gray residue of scorched boils. Gray spaces were safe; no Kree burrow was ever more than a few meters from a crop of their primary fare. Each of the five cities on Tora sat inside such a sooty ring, islands burnt into a sea of scarlet.

Today they traveled near the edge of Echo's ring, entering Kree territory more than a dozen klicks from the hole young Gretchen discovered yesterday. The gray landscape developed ginger highlights, sporadic clumps of boils that refused to wither completely away. The highlights grew denser, full streaks against the brown-gray lunar soil.

The damn beasts were out there, listening to the engines, hearing not with ears but with their entire bodies. Stealth had no place in today's plan. This was no search-and-scorch patrol; it was a hunting party with a mission to seek and destroy.

They reached their assigned coordinates and deployed on foot in teams of four. Ashia cursed her luck, teaming with her lieutenant, one rookie, and that greenhorn Gretchen. How was she going to bag boils with an officer and two twitchy novices at her back? How were they going to survive a Kree encounter? She kept one hand on her rifle, the other on a gas grenade.

"Gas then shoot," Ashia told the rookie, unbidden, as if trainees hadn't heard the mantra a million times at the academy. "Throw short. Shoot for the elbow to disable, the throat to kill."

"Would you shut up?" the lieutenant hissed. "This ain't a classroom and no one needs a refresher course."

"I...I could use one," Gretchen said.

The other girl nodded agreement.

A report came from another foursome. "We got a hole!"

It certainly seemed to be a Kree hole. It had all the characteristic signs. There were no boils near the entrance, all scraped away and consumed by the cave's occupants. The soil at the mouth had been recently disturbed. Ashia had encountered hundreds of Kree holes over her twelve years of service, but never one this obvious. Kree were sightless, but a few centuries dealing with humans taught them how to cover their tracks. It was almost as if they wanted...

"It's a decoy."

Ashia caught hell during debriefing. The entire mission had been scrapped on her word, nevermind that her rank was insufficient to decide her own breakfast. How did she know the hole was a fake? What kind of trap were the Kree setting? On whose authority did she offer her opinion? The same questions came over and over. They kept asking because they knew she was right. Ashia was never wrong outside the walls.

The conference concluded with a minimal sanction and an offer of promotion, neither the first she had seen. She paid both the same heed. What the hell did she want with officer's stripes?

It was getting dark by the time she departed the base and entered the city proper. She found Hector waiting for her. "I have submitted for my test," he declared as an orator might to a crowd that was not there. "Where is your wonder-stud?"

What was worse, men or Kree? "I asked him to do nothing until I returned. Unlike some males, he knows how to show proper deference to a lady."

Hector snorted. "A lady? I don't recall you being so ladylike during the conception."

"Of course you don't. You weren't there." Kicking, scratching, begging him to stop were no longer considered ladylike?

She allowed Hector to follow her to Kurtas's dormitory. Kurtas saw them coming and met them outside. Her son's paranoia was so predictable.

"I thought you were coming alone," Kurtas said.

She knew why he was angry. It was the reason she had allowed Hector to tag along. She patted a hand not so subtly against a pocket. "It's all business tonight."

Kurtas acknowledged the pat with a defeated nod. He believed she had the boils, he would submit to the test. But what would it say?

It was late enough that the planet filled the lunar sky before Ashia and Kurtas could speak alone. Kurtas did most of that speaking. "So where is it?"

Ashia lowered her eyes.

"I knew it." He kicked over a chair. "How could you do this to me?"

"I was never alone out there, not an instant. It wasn't possible."

"But me beating Hector on a paternity test of his own son, that is possible?" He pushed his palms up his face and across his scalp. "I don't know how I'm going to make it through the night."

"What, you think Hector is going to kill you in your sleep?"

Kurtas released what could have been a wheeze or a laugh. "Hector? What do I care of Hector? If I die in the night, the pain killed me."

"The pain? What about—"

"I told you, I had an order. A big one. I filled it."

Ashia gaped. "You sold it all? Can you get some back?"

"It's Puff, Mother, it doesn't work that way."

"Don't call me—"

"It doesn't matter what I call you. Mother, woman, Ashia, Brutus…" He coughed into his hand. She watched the flecks of blood strike his fingers.

"Could you buy some off someone else?"

"Because they'd sell to me?"

"Then I can buy it. Just a dose or two, to pull you through."

Kurtas shook his head.

"Maybe one of your buyers that owes you a favor?"

"You better go." He opened the door. "This is going to get uglier before it gets pretty."

"I'm not going to let you die."

"It's just pain, woman." With the door open, he was back in character. "I'll be there tomorrow for the results." His hand quaked as he ushered her out.

The magistrate's chamber was cold when Ashia entered the next morning. She was the first to arrive. Hector would be there soon. He didn't matter. What shape would Kurtas be in? She should have checked on him.

The chamber door opened. Hector entered, followed directly by Kurtas. He looked tired but seemed otherwise fine, even a shade ruddier than usual. How would anyone believe a boy that pale sired Elias?

"I see all parties are present," said the magistrate, "so let's get this show on the road." She tapped at her console. Her round face puckered.

"Well," the magistrate said as she stared at her display, "this is a new one for me. Congratulations, gentlemen, you are both the father."

Hector stood. "What nonsense is this?"

"Take a seat or I will have you removed."

Hector sat reluctantly, apparently cowed by true authority. On Tora, men did not question the authority of a woman when she had it. Not twice.

The magistrate smirked ever so slightly before continuing. "I am neither a doctor nor scientist, but I have presided over enough paternity disputes to know that you both fit the parameters of decisive paternity. Hector is a ninety-four percent match; Kurtas is…eighty-five. You two aren't brothers by any chance?" No reaction. "I thought not. Perhaps distant cousins? With the history of this colony, anything as possible." If she suspected any relation to Ashia, she provided no hint.

"The test has a listed error near five percent," the magistrate continued. "My personal suspicions aside, I can make no binding judgment from the data before me."

"This is preposterous—"

The magistrate straightened her posture and glared at Hector. "That's twice."

"Ninety-four percent, you said it yourself." The words were under his breath.

"Tora was established as a mining colony, not a metropolis. On a core planet, sure, you could get a perfect result. If you believe you can break the Kree blockade to get to one, be my guest. Otherwise, you can wait for a screening of the mother."

"Screening?" Ashia had almost dared be pleased with the magistrate's report. Fool. "Why would I have to be screened?"

The magistrate shrugged. "No medical facility on Tora is equipped for more than general genetic testing. Prior conflicts, mostly involving brothers, have been resolved by scanning the mother and eliminating her matches from the child's sequence. Process of elimination. It's not exactly precision science, but the docs stand behind it. Good enough for me."

"So scan the woman," Hector said. "We do it now."

"You really have your ego in a twist over this," Ashia said.

"You credit this bald adolescent with siring my son? It's principle."

"It's lunacy," Kurtas said, speaking for the first time. "I don't care whose kid it is."

The magistrate sighed. "It is a matter of concern for future propagation. It should not concern a male so much, the paternity of a single child. Still, we don't want genetic disease and weakness infecting the colony."

Kurtas glared at Ashia. She pretended not to notice.

"The mother will report for testing within the next twenty hours. Now leave, all of you. I have more important matters than your sordid affairs."

Hector stormed out, bumping Kurtas with his shoulder like a schoolyard bully as he passed.

Ashia caught Kurtas outside the chamber. "You look good," she said, hoping her motherly concern sounded like a lover's interest. "After last night—"

"A friend shared with me," Kurtas said. He sounded both relieved and angry. "A client, a woman. She heard I had sired a strong boy. She gave me what I needed in exchange for what she needed."

Ashia pulled him aside by the elbow. "You mated with her? During her cycle?"

"I wouldn't have had to if you had kept your promise."

"And if she conceives? What then?"

"It won't be the first child born ill. Thanks to you, there may be many. I am becoming popular."

"Play hard to get," Ashia whispered harshly. "Wait a week before you submit. For Messiah sake, don't let the woman pick the timing."

"I did what I had to. I'd be writhing on the floor without her help."

"Who was she?"

Kurtas pulled his arm free and walked away without answering.

"So we're back to patrols? Just like that?" Gretchen said as streaks of red passed beside their scout pod. "What about the monstrous hole?"

Ashia shrugged. "There's nothing in that hole. Sonar confirms it's not deep enough to hide anything. It was a rush job to distract us from something else."

"But what?"

That was the question. Two hundred years ago, the Kree had used a diversion and decimated most of Tora's military force including ninety percent of the colony's males. On what scale were they plotting this time? The only thing to do was keep looking.

The pair of scout pods pulled to a stop where their last patrol had ended. There had been reassignments made in light of recent losses. Lieutenant wet-ears had taken over Ashia's squad and brought two of her fellows with her. Now true combat veterans, Ashia considered the change an asset.

The return to basic search-and-scorch patterns should have made it easy to steal a few boils into the can, but Lt. Wet-Ears had them arranged in tight formation and recent events left the women twitchy, constantly looking to their squadmates for support. For over two hours Ashia found no chance to make a grab. Finally she lost patience, broke formation and slid behind a boulder to make her move. She twisted open the canister and pressed a cluster of boils inside. She was out of line for mere seconds. She turned to resume her place only to find she wasn't alone.

It was Gretchen. The girl's mouth stayed open, her eyes alternating from Ashia's face to the open canister in her fist.

Ashia screwed the lid back in place and stowed the false grenade with the real ones. "Can I help you, Private?"

Gretchen's eyes were still on the fake grenade. She did not speak.

"We better get back in formation." Ashia's attempt to sound friendly failed. She walked toward the patrol, coaxing Gretchen by the elbow as she passed.

The novice followed several steps before saying, "Those are for Kurtas?"

Ashia stopped and faced the girl, looked into her eyes. Gretchen looked sad, betrayed, defeated. For one fleeting instant Ashia considered telling her everything. About Kurtas, Elias, Hector…even Tam. It would feel good to say the words to someone other than Kurtas. It didn't matter if Gretchen told the whole moon; the truth had to be said.

Then the moment passed. Gretchen already knew too much, more than Ashia had dared believe anyone could know. She considered killing the girl, a quick round through the chest. A friendly fire incident attributable to the stress of recent events. It would be a significant rip, but nothing career ending.

The thought made Ashia sick, partially because she believed it might truly come to that. But not now. Not yet.

"Everyone knows he did not sire your son," Gretchen said, her voice like a sigh of despair. "Did he bed you in exchange for boils? Or was it just an exchange for Puff?"

"An exchange for…" Then it was clear. Ashia looked the direction of Echo, as if doing so would reveal her son. "It was you that shared his bed last night."

Gretchen straightened. "He needed me. I came through."

Her Puff had come through. This colored the novice a new shade. A Puff addict fixated on her dealer; a kindred spirit to her son. Would she tell what she had seen and expose her own addiction?

"Did he...are you...?" Ashia's eyes fell to the girl's belly.

Gretchen shook her head, retreated a step. "I was ill as a child. They removed...I cannot. Please, don't tell Kurtas."

Ashia bit her lip. Kurtas would not be exposed through this girl, not unless she spoke. "We should get back before we are missed."

Gretchen nodded just as the sound of gunfire began.

The two warriors exchanged startled glances before racing back toward their unit. They crested a low rise to find their squad in a basin a full hundred fifty meters ahead. The formation was splintered, women ducking behind rocks and trees for whatever cover they could find. A ribbon of pink smoke sailed through the air. Ashia followed its arc and saw the enemy.

Scientists classified the Kree as humanoid, a designation Ashia had always considered generous. They possessed all the pieces of a human body by name, but everything served a different purpose. Their heads were little more than glorified noses, four independently sealable nostrils tucked under a thick awning of bone and tusk.

The things' arms were as tall as their whole body, reminiscent of a gorilla in how they walked, but on palms rather than knuckles. The three digits of the hands were more toes than fingers; they folded open for walking and closed against a thumb-like nub for clumsy grasping.

What should have been its two legs were short and multi-jointed — practically tentacles — each culminating in what resembled a six-limbed starfish. These feet rather than the hands were responsible for Kree technology, and it was the feet that wielded their plasma throwers, implements that made the humans' flamers look like cigarette lighters.

A small choking sound came from Gretchen. It was the first the girl had seen one of these monstrosities in person. The young always reacted that way, but they usually recovered quickly.

There was only one Kree visible, but there were sure to be others lurking. They never struck alone, always in numbers and always in ambush.

Ashia stepped into Gretchen's eyeline. "We flank him, distract enough to let the others mount a full assault. There will be more; stay sharp."

Gretchen followed numbly, a stunned dog trotting on its leash. "It's our fault, isn't it?" she whined. "We were out of formation. We..."

Ashia stopped, pulled Gretchen into a crouch at her side. "If we were with them, we'd be just as pinned as they are. The other Kree are likely executing this same maneuver. We have to be quick, efficient, and quiet. The others' gunfire should mask our footfalls for a while, but Kree are one giant ear. Step lightly and keep moving. If you see one, gas it."

Gretchen's eyes trembled in their sockets. Had she understood? No time to find out. Ashia resumed motion. Gretchen followed, not stealthy but not loud. Good girl. She might just survive long enough to tattle.

They closed to about seventy-five meters, well inside the Kree's scent range. Hopefully it was distracted enough not to notice. The gas was good for that.

The only cover nearby were a few shrubs that would never withstand the plasma bursts and would impede neither sound nor scent. So Ashia stood in the open as she sized up the lone alien.

Three of its nostrils were sealed, shields against the choking gas. Good. One peeking nostril might smell them coming but could not triangulate them, the same way a one-eyed human had difficulties with depth perception. Unfortunately the gunfire had slowed to only an occasional pop. So much for sound cover. Even from this range, Ashia could see the sensitive bristles standing erect over the Kree's gray-brown body, listening.

Ashia signaled for Gretchen to freeze, plucked a grenade from her belt, pulled the pin.

The Kree faced them. Damn. All four nostrils unfolded. They were spotted.

Ashia threw the grenade. It landed twenty meters short. She had expected the monster to charge, but it hadn't. At least the gas would obscure their aroma to the olfactory-dependant enemy. It would be fighting by sound, its nostrils tight again to ward off the new gas.

A Kree could fixate on weapons fire after only three rounds on automatic. Ashia flipped her weapon to single-fire. Gretchen imitated.

"Ashia! That you?" Her radio. She couldn't speak without betraying her position. Even the earpiece might prove too loud. She pulled the field mirror from her belt and flashed confirmation to her squadmates in the valley below.

"Do you see any others?" the lieutenant said, panic staining the edges of the words. "Are they surrounding us?"

Ashia surveyed the terrain as long as she dared. The one confirmed enemy remained behind the cloud. Still no sign of the ambush. Ashia mirror-flashed her uncertainty.

"We're going to make a run for the pods. Can you cover?"

She flashed negative.

"We're going. We can't stay in this barrel."

Ashia repeated her negative flash. Damn fools. The other Kree must be securing the scout pods. Where else would they be?

The lieutenant ignored her. Ashia saw the ten figures start their retreat in the basin below. She wanted to shout at the lieutenant, to scold her for her cowardice. To do so was suicide. She had a Kree to deal with; the officer would wait.

Pop-pop-pop.

Gretchen fired into the smoke, blind shots. The lieutenant's panic was contagious. Now the novice was giving away their position.

"Move!" Ashia sprinted parallel to the wall of smoke. Gretchen also ran but directly away from the Kree's last confirmed position. The mistake left the girl in the line of fire. The main plasma burst was short, but she did not escape the splash ring.

Gretchen screamed as the burn bit calf. She collapsed.

Ashia froze. Gretchen was a sitting duck. At least Ashia might use the girl's cries to hide her own position. She flipped another grenade a few yards to cover her scent and waited.

The Kree emerged from the cloud and lurched unevenly toward Gretchen's prone and writhing body. Two nostrils unfolded, confirming its target's location. It resealed and continued its advance.

So close. Thirty meters. Twenty. Fifteen. Ashia stopped breathing. Every hair on the beast was stiff and vibrating. It was so close Ashia could see its many scars. An old specimen that had seen much battle. Not so unlike Ashia herself. A veteran, alone on a hill against a sworn enemy.

Ten meters.

Ashia would have to breathe soon. Could it hear the accelerated rhythm of her heart? It was now or never. The moment she moved, it would hear her. She had to make it one smooth motion — level the weapon and fire. One shot. Disabling the beast at this range would buy her nothing. This had to be a kill shot. The head was the most vulnerable, a low trajectory, through a nostril and into the brainstem. Now or never.

But it was Gretchen that stopped screaming and started firing.

The Kree took a hit to the right arm. It reeled and charged Gretchen, limping.

Ashia raised her weapon and squeezed off two shots.

The Kree landed on Gretchen. Limbs splayed, body limp. It was dead.

Ashia left her wounded compatriot beneath the hulking corpse — what better cover could there be? — and secured the area. No evidence of any other Kree. She was about to declare the scene clear when the lieutenant piped through.

"Ashia, we have the pods. Can you report your status?"

No ambush? Had they really stumbled across a lone Kree? A rogue? An outcast? Amazing the thing could survive this close to a city like Echo. Could it have dug the diversionary hole itself?

Since there were no other targets, the next priority was to call in medevac for Gretchen. Ashia fingered her transmitter to report, but said nothing.

She would report the all clear, Gretchen would be whisked to the hospital, and Ashia would follow her there for mandatory testing. To Hector go the spoils. What of Kurtas? Elias?

Ashia released the button and returned to Gretchen's side. The girl was covered in Kree from shoulder to burnt toe. Some of the beast's blood had spilled on her face. Red blood, iron-based. What else might Ashia have in common with this creature?

She turned Gretchen's face to her. The girl struggled to focus. Her eyes widened, her breath quickened. She pushed at the enormous Kree corpse with both hands to no avail.

"How much do you know?" Ashia said, half to herself. "What have you guessed?"

Gretchen tried to speak. "Please…no…"

Ashia pressed a finger to the young lips. Her other hand relieved the girl of several gas grenades and all of her emergency provisions, a month worth to a cautious eater.

"Relax, greenhorn," Ashia said. "I'm not going to kill you. I need you. My boys need you."

Gretchen's eyebrows bunched. She didn't understand.

"Ask Kurtas. He will explain. He's yours now. You understand him in ways his mother never could. Take him as your own. You're the war hero; I am but a casualty."

Gretchen struggled to sit up, grabbed Ashia's wrist.

Ashia caressed the girl's hand. "Save your strength for the radio call.

And I need you to do one more thing: Elias will need a mother, you and Kurtas will need a son." She tucked the hollow canister into Gretchen's belt. "My family is yours now. Take care of them."

Ashia stood, turned, and walked away. She refused to look back. She was leaving so much behind, but the lies stayed behind with all of it. She hiked to the small hole Gretchen had found a few days earlier — the rogue Kree's home, now Ashia's. A home without walls.

Things were simpler outside the walls.

Chasers

Sebastian's organs squeezed into his pelvis as he accelerated past point-one. He had a good feeling this time. This catch was going to be his.

He could see his objective ahead of him, the enormous Drifter-class colony ship *Calypso* barreling through space on her inertial journey from Earth to Terra III. Since she carried no fuel for deceleration, *Calypso* would travel through space forever without Chasers like Sebastian. It was the job of a Chaser to run down Drifters and fill their tanks. The job had sounded easy when he signed with Mulligan Mining eight months ago. But despite nine arrivals since then, Sebastian has not made one catch.

Calypso was a slow Drifter at a mere point-13 c. Surely he could catch that. His Skeeter was designed to reach point-2, faster and more maneuverable than any other company's ships. Yet what advantages Skeeters held in speed and agility they sacrificed in capacity. Even if he caught the Drifter, it took a total of three Skeeters to fill her.

Sebastian ran a scan of *Calypso*. Leonard was already docked. That was too fast for him to have waited for the Drifter's beacon; he must have taken his Skeeter out without confirmation a Drifter was coming in. Lucky. Blind patrols were expensive gambles, especially on a Chaser's budget. The exorbitant price of fuel on Earth was the primary reason Drifter-class colonizers dominated the colonization market, and a booming fuel industry made Terra III the most popular destination. Like most things, it boiled down to money.

A pair of blips appeared on Sebastian's nav-screen. Two ships were approaching from behind. The tiny blip indicated the presence of another Skeeter, the third they'd need to fill the *Calypso*. The larger blip was an

Essex Bus, a hundred-percent capacity tanker from a rival fuel company. Rather, Essex was *the* rival of Mulligan. Both Sebastian and the other Skeeter would have to beat this Bus if Mulligan was going to make the sale. If the Bus docked first, the sale would go to Essex. One Bus could do the job of three Skeeters, assuming it could get to the colony ship first.

Sebastian pushed his engines harder.

The big blip was moving fast for a ship its size. It drew closer until Sebastian could see it through his canopy. It was more than three times the size of his little Skeeter and was now careening at point-16 c. "Damn," Sebastian whispered as he was overtaken, "I thought Busses maxed out at point-15." It was the reason Sebastian had signed with Mulligan instead of Essex: the need for speed. Busses just weren't meant to go that fast. But even one percent of the speed of light could mean the difference between a bonus check and a long flight back to port. If a Chaser could finagle a little extra zip out of his ship, he did. Apparently this Bus pilot was a finagler.

Sebastian adjusted his fuel ratios and pushed his engines even harder. The ship began to vibrate around him. Still the Bus pulled away. "One Skeeter already on and Essex is going to get the sale anyway," Sebastian said. He started the calculations for his return to port.

"You ain't giving up, are you?" a voice croaked across the closed-circuit communicator. Closed-circuit meant it was another Mulligan pilot.

"Repeat?" Sebastian replied.

"Bas, that you?" Only one person ever called him Bas.

"Roger, this is Sebastian. What's your twenty, Wild?"

"I'll be on your screen in a shake."

"Don't bother. I was just passed by a Bus going point-16."

"Isn't Freebird already on?" Wild meant Leonard. He refused to call anyone by their actual name, including himself. He wasn't born with the name Johnny Wild, but no one knew anything different to call him. Besides, he lived up to it.

"Roger that, Leonard has already docked with the *Calypso*. I'm the next closest Skeeter at—" Sebastian checked his numbers, "—one hundred eighty thousand kilometers."

"You still think like a kid in the belly of one of those Drifters," Wild said. "We use mega-meters out here. That's a hundred eighty m&m's. You're right on top of her!"

"I'm not moving fast enough. If that Essex pilot is any good, he'll be docked before we get there."

"That Essex pilot is Old Harold."

Sebastian's heart sank. Old Harold had been chasing ships longer than Sebastian had been eating solid food, and he hadn't lost a step. If any Essex pilot was good, Harold was. "I might as well just head back."

"You just leave Harold to me," Wild said. "Get your ass up to that Drifter and we'll make this catch."

"Where did you say you were?"

"Look up."

Sebastian did, just in time to see a streak of pink pass above his canopy. Only Wild was man enough to fly a pink Skeeter. Most guys flew some macho combination of black and red or blue. Wild's ship was hot pink and no one gave him any crap about it. At least not twice.

Sebastian screamed an expletive into his communicator. "You must be close to point-3. Are you crazy?"

"Not crazy, just wild. This ain't no friendly game out here. If you can't take it, move on."

If you can't take it, move on. The third rule of Chaserdom. The second rule awarded the sale to the first company to dock a full load of fuel. The first rule: Chasers will catch every Drifter at any cost.

Wild began his deceleration as soon as he passed Sebastian. In the minute they'd been talking, Sebastian had closed to about five thousand kilometers — five m&m's — and started his own deceleration. Catching up to a Drifter was simple enough, just straight-line flight as fast as you dared to go. Docking was quite another. The maneuver required timing, finesse, precise calculation, and constant reference to the Skeeter's entire battery of sensors.

Something on the screen caught Sebastian's attention, a blip far in front of the Drifter. It was Wild. The fool had shot right past the Drifter before managing to drop his speed. Now he was slowing to allow the *Calypso* to creep up on him, effectively approaching the Drifter from the front along its port side, backward.

Old Harold was already working the port side. His Bus was perfectly matching *Calypso*'s pace from a distance of two kilometers and was sliding laterally toward the docking cap. There was only one cap on that side and Wild wasn't about to let Harold take it.

Small as a Skeeter may seem in comparison to other ships, it still hauled a third of a Drifter's fuel capacity, requiring it to be nearly a quarter kilometer in diameter. Sebastian tried not to think of these specs as Wild edged his ship into the rapidly shrinking gap between Harold's much larger Bus and the absolutely enormous Drifter. And he was doing it backward.

Harold's Bus paused as the Skeeter slipped into the crack. He even backed off a little, for a moment. Then his voice came across the open-band communicator. "That must be Johnny."

"None other," Wild responded.

"No one else would try a stunt that extraordinarily stupid."

"You still plan on scooting over here?"

"Hey, you know the rules," Harold said. The Bus began to nudge laterally again, closing on the Drifter and on Wild in between. "It's tough competition out here. If you can't take it…"

A light on Sebastian's panel flashed twice then remained lit. Fuel lock on *Calypso*'s port side.

"…then move on," Wild concluded for Harold. Wild was on.

A tense moment passed with Harold's Bus less than a quarter kilometer from Wild, a Skeeter-width. Finally Harold rolled his ship toward the Drifter's belly. He was beaten.

"I'm on," Wild announced over the Mulligan channel. "Your turn, Bas."

Sebastian had been too enthralled with Wild's psychotic maneuver to pay attention to his own progress. He had inadvertently slipped past the docking cap during the excitement. "Uh, working on it." He kicked his retros and gradually allowed the cap to catch up with him. He was less than a kilometer off the Drifter now, moments away from his first catch.

A proximity alarm interrupted Sebastian's thoughts. "What the—" The Drifter was factored into the navigational equations and shouldn't trigger any alarms. But it wasn't the Drifter; Harold was repaying Wild's favor on Sebastian, only the gap on this side was certainly not wide enough for a Bus to squeeze through. He was going to sideswipe Sebastian's Skeeter.

Sebastian flinched. He kicked in a lateral thruster and slid away from the cap. Harold was docked forty seconds later.

"Ha ha!" Harold screeched over the open-band. "Better luck next time kid. This isn't a game of touch football, you know. If you can't take it, move on."

It was a long month that passed while Sebastian waited for the next colony ship to arrive. He avoided all the Chaser bars and hangouts, even

Burnout's. He didn't respond to the dinner invitations Wild's wife sent. He just couldn't face Wild or any other Chaser after what had happened. It made for a very secluded existence on a Chaser port. He didn't even pick up his stipend check in fear that it might be his last. It was Sebastian's fault Mulligan lost out on the *Calypso* sale. Wild and Leonard lost bonuses because of him. Harold added another notch to his already obnoxious résumé because of him.

Sebastian spent the next weeks psyching himself up for the coming chase. When the next Drifter beacon finally registered, Sebastian stepped into the bustling decon room convinced this catch would be his.

"Where you been, Bas?" asked a middle-aged man wearing nothing but sunglasses. It was Wild. "Hiding out? You're not gonna wrap this one up for Old Harold and those Essex goons like you did the last one, are you?"

"No, this one's got my name on it," Sebastian boasted as he kicked off his boots. "Besides, that old coot cut in on me at point-13. I didn't feel like playing bumper cars at a seventh the speed of light!"

Wild selected a sterile flight suit from his locker, broke the seal, and stuffed a cigar into the breast pocket. "Old Harold always plays rough with newbies, but he didn't want to ding his boat neither. Nudge back next time, see who's who."

Sebastian stopped unbuttoning his shirt long enough to scoff at the suggestion. "My little Skeeter against an Essex Bus? He has more than three times a Skeeter's mass! That's not a game of chicken anymore; it's a game of cuckoo."

"How many catches you got, Bas?"

Sebastian stepped into a steam stall, ignoring the question.

"Exactly!" Wild called after him. "There's a reason we fly Skeeters. Gotta be fast. Gotta be fearless. Gotta be crazier than the other guy. If not, go drive a Bus for Essex."

Sebastian shook his head as the chemical steam enveloped him. The cloud was subsiding when he finally called out to Wild, "This catch will be ours. I'll hold it for you."

"Just like you held the last one, tyke? I appreciate it!" The voice was not Wild's.

Wild was gone, replaced by the silver-haired, heavyset arch-criminal of the Chaser industry. "Harold," Sebastian growled.

"A few more like last month's and you'll be on the Essex wall of fame,"

Old Harold laughed. "Right under my picture."

"Great, now I need another steam bath. I thought the chemicals were supposed to kill parasites like you."

Harold made a tsk-tsk sound. "Boy, someone should teach you respect for your elders."

"You got the elderly part right."

"Don't spew your venom at me." Harold raised his hands, pantomiming innocence. "*I* didn't back off a catch because of a little competition. If that Drifter had waited for you to drum up the courage to dock, it might have coasted through deep space forever. If you can't take it, move on."

Sebastian's retort was too slow in forming and never quite escaped his lips. Instead he stepped into the white room to don his flight suit.

Sebastian knew Wild would make it to this Drifter. Mulligan could always count on Wild. He just hoped they could count on Sebastian for once. And who else? Leonard again? Doubtful. Not that it mattered. As long as Mulligan made a sale, the first three Skeeters would go home with a bonus — both in cash and Mulligan stock. Everyone else would just go home.

Sebastian sealed his suit. He was going to make this catch. He stepped out into the hangar to prepare his ship.

The outpost shrank away as Sebastian pushed his Skeeter past point-one. The G-forces were almost enough to squeeze Old Harold from his head. He soon found himself amidst a dozen other ships, all streaking forth in hopes of landing a deal with the incoming vessel. He recognized five other Skeeters, one Essex full-load tanker (not Harold's), and a couple horticulturalist vendors hoping the transport might have a damaged eco-garden. The rest of the vessels were most likely service merchants from other outposts: prostitutes, real estate brokers, military recruiters, and missionaries all hoping to get a leg-up on the competition by striking before the colonists reached the planet.

This Drifter was moving just under point-16, a much better pace than the last as far as Skeeter pilots were concerned. Faster Chasers catch faster Drifters.

Sebastian checked his gauges. He was already past point-13, less than three hundredths from matching pace. Still not close enough. He pushed the engines to red as the careening Drifter started to pass the cluster of hopefuls. He was already close, close enough that he felt like he could reach out and touch the Drifter. Yet it might as well have been a million mega-meters away. Any attempt to dock with such a speed differential would rip his tiny ship to shreds.

The field of crafts thinned and scattered as all seventeen kilometers of colony ship passed. The giant Drifter was little more than a speck in space by the time Sebastian had matched its speed. He pushed harder. His whole vessel began to clatter with the effort, but he couldn't afford to back off. He needed to catch that ship.

His dial reached point-23. He'd only reached this speed once in the simulator and never in an actual ship. Sebastian's knuckles were white. "Wild would be proud," he said through his rattling teeth.

Suddenly, there was another ship on top of him. It streaked past as if Sebastian's recklessly fast Skeeter were standing still.

"That you, Bas?" Wild's voice chimed over the noise of the cockpit. "Movin pretty good for a newbie. You might just catch this one!" Sebastian was too flustered to respond.

"Relax, I see you coming," Wild assured. "There ain't no one else up here. You can probably coast her in from there."

"You sure?" Sebastian couldn't afford to screw this up.

"I ever steered you wrong?"

He hadn't.

Sebastian cut his engines, diffusing the vibrations with them. His inertia closed the gap quickly. He fired his retros to reduce his velocity enough to avoid shooting past his objective.

Every nerve in Sebastian's body writhed as he eased his ship toward the docking cap. This was where he'd blown it last time. The mere thought of Harold's Bus muscling over on him made his palms sweat. But Harold wasn't here. No one else was here. This was Sebastian's catch to make or lose.

He wiped his face. He had to focus! After all, if he couldn't take it, he should just move on. But Sebastian didn't want to move on; he wanted this catch.

Long minutes passed while Sebastian edged toward the Drifter. He heard the chafing of metal on metal as he moved too close too quickly. The ship lurched tangentially. He slapped at his thrusters in desperation. The next sound was louder. *Chunk!* He was docked.

Sebastian collapsed in his seat, relishing the unfamiliar sensation of success. His heart raced; his hands were numb. "I'm on," he finally gasped, still gasping from the rush. "I'm on."

"Congrats, kiddo," Wild said over the Mulligan channel. "Come on in. I'm talking to the captain. I think we may have a sale here. Ray-Ray was right behind you."

Sebastian frowned at the fueling hatch. He had actually thought he'd beaten Wild. He should have known better.

The bio-scan flashed green, indicating Sebastian carried no bacteria that could infect the passengers. Most of the colonists had been born en route. Generation ships like this one did not react well to foreign microbes. The pressure between the hatches equalized and Sebastian slid into the massive vessel.

The interior was unremarkable, as had been the exterior short of its sheer immensity. If you had seen one Drifter, you'd seen them all. Being born on one made them that much less fascinating to Sebastian, especially this vast network of dim service tubes. They were more akin to drainage pipes than passageways. Sebastian crawled up into the ship. His stomach protested the artificial gravity as he entered, but he managed to stifle his reaction.

His senses had fully adapted by the time he arrived in the captain's lounge. Wild was already waiting with the captain, an older lady with lonely eyes and thinning hair. She was likely from the ship's first freefall generation. Sebastian felt a twinge of disappointment. Every Chaser knew the story of the beautiful gen-three pilot Wild had encountered, wooed, and married four years back. The pair now had a sex life that belied all the clichés about marriage and two daughters that thought their daddy hung the moons. It was a fairytale every Chaser hoped to emulate. This captain didn't seem a sufficient candidate.

"Sebastian," Wild said, stirring him from his disappointment. Sebastian had never heard his full name escape Wild's mouth. "This is Captain Erika Braxton, our newest client."

"Gentlemen," the captain smiled, "welcome aboard Drifter *Eternity*."

Wild toasted the welcome with his flask and relit his cigar. "This looks like quite a ship," he commented diplomatically. Wild could reportedly negotiate price with anyone in the galaxy. Sebastian had never before had the opportunity to watch him work. His eyes actually twinkled as he spoke. "How many passengers you carry?"

"We have quarters for about six thousand," Captain Braxton said importantly, "almost all full, though we started with about eleven hundred. Plus we have a few passengers in special transport."

Wild's cigar quivered. "Special transport? You mean Frosties?"

She nodded.

The mere mention of Frosties drained the blood from Sebastian's extremities. He'd heard too many stories about faulty cryo-units and premature thawing. It just didn't seem worth the risk to him. Most colonists felt the same way, accepting a life in the confines of a colony ship in exchange for a future on Terra III for their children's children. To most colonists, anything was better than Earth. But not cryo-travel.

Captain Braxton smiled, misinterpreting the Chasers' reactions as interest. "They are very important passengers. Dr. Steinen and his associates are the minds behind a new system of entirely fuel-free colonization." Wild's eye developed a tiny tremor as she spoke. "As I understand it, they will use a series of magnetic and gravitonic accelerators to propel colony ships to nearly one-half c. Trajectory will be calculated precisely enough that the ship can be dropped into another series of magnets on this end. That receiver is what Steinen and company are here to build.

"It's supposed to be a mega-trillion dollar project, but its impact on colonization will be tremendous. Trips will be fast enough that young men and women who depart from Earth will be able to see Terra III in their lifetime. The savings on fuel alone should quickly offset the initial investment.

"Earth-side has already set up the accelerator. My father even saw part of it on his way out of the Sol system. The sequence begins just beyond the asteroid belt and reaches beyond the orbit of Pluto." A comparable arrangement in the Terra III system would reach twice as far out as Sebastian had ever ventured.

"How many of your passengers are involved in this project?" Wild asked, most of the sociability faded from his tone and the twinkle extinguished.

"This is a corporate-sponsored vessel. Most of the colonists are trained to either service the catcher or assist in its construction, but my cryostatic passengers are the engineers who designed the original slingshot. The entire project is their baby. When we arrive, they'll be in charge. They trusted no one else to the task, preferring to hibernate so they could see their dream to fruition. They expect the catcher to be complete within the next forty years." The gleam in her eye betrayed her excitement at the prospect.

Wild's eye, on the other hand, seemed to cast its own shadow. "What will this project do to the fuel industry here, T3-side?"

The woman wrinkled her already pruny nose as she thought a long moment on the issue. "I imagine ships will be needed to maintain the accelerator," she responded slowly, searching for each word. "Plus whatever intra-system travel goes on here. There may even be an occasional old-style colony ship. But otherwise…" Her gaze dropped to the floor as the thought faded away without completion.

Sebastian's communicator interrupted the exchange. "This is Fisher. I'm on." He had somehow edged out Rayburn. That meant the third Skeeter was ready. The other fuel ships, beaten, decelerated and headed back to port. Sebastian had earned his first bonus.

"Sorry, but yer too slow!" Fisher taunted over the open-band at the defeated Chasers. "Don't like it? Move on!" Sebastian and Wild excused themselves abruptly and returned to their ships to begin the fueling sequence.

Sebastian ran his fueling checklist. The concept of this gravitonic catcher rattled through his head, making it difficult to focus on the process at hand. He did his best to double- and triple-check each step lest his first catch explode from a loose seal or a faulty hose. Sudden decompression of a fuel tank would be bad news — news he would never hear. He had just finished sealing the last connection when his communicator signaled a secure transmission.

"Bas?" Wild whispered, "How many catches you got?"

Sebastian started the warm-up cycle on the pumps. "Thank you for reminding me that this is my first. Why, do I get hazed tonight or something?"

"Know how many I got?"

"Wild, you have more catches than anyone but Old Harold," Sebastian said. "What is this, ninety-six?" Wild had been part of every Mulligan sale in the past four years.

Wild released a half-laugh. "Sixty-four…plus this one." There was a long silence. "That's a lot of bonuses. A lot of Mulligan stock."

Sebastian grunted agreement.

"My family has to live off that stock when I'm gone. Thought it would be a great start. Not so sure now."

"What are you talking about?" Sebastian threw a switch and his system started to hum. "You plan on being gone sometime soon?" Chasers had a tendency to predict their own deaths. Lots of adrenaline junkies did, especially after endorphins faded from a chase. This was nothing new, or so Sebastian thought.

"I aim to be round a while," said Wild. "Starting to wonder which'll be gone first, me or Mulligan. I can't leave my family with nothing."

"Is this about that catcher thing? It will be decades before that takes over, probably half a century. You won't have to see Mulligan shrivel."

"My girls will."

Another long moment of dead air.

"What are you saying? You aren't planning to defrost anyone?"

"No, Bas," Wild said, a little too calmly. "But I can't help them kill Mulligan. I can't."

"Okay Wild, you're scaring me now. Just get your load in and we'll go hit Burnout's for a nice bottomless pint. My treat."

"You don't get it, do you Bas?"

The conversation was interrupted. "Wild," Fisher squawked over the Mulligan circuit, "something wrong? My readings say you aren't pushing anything in. In fact, your pumps are reading cold. Everything okay? You're slower than the kid today."

Sebastian confirmed Fisher's report with his own readings; there were no vibrations originating from Wild's ship. He hadn't even begun to warm up his pumps.

Sebastian switched back to the private channel, deafening Fisher to the conversation. "Wild, are you nuts? The other Skeeters are gone. Everyone's gone. No other Chaser is going to make it here in time. If we're going get ourselves back to the port then we need to get this ship full and decelerating within the next six hours, preferably three. If you're cold, we're talking that long just to get your fuel in her."

"Bas... I just can't."

"If we don't fill this ship, you will be murdering every one of these passengers."

"They can live long, happy lives inside this ship," Wild said coolly. "It's all they know."

"Forget the passengers, then. If you go back to the outpost with a full load, God knows what kind of penalties you'll get slapped with."

"Nothing will happen if no one knows."

"Right, no one's going to notice that your tank is still full?"

"Who says the tank will be full?" Wild's docking clamps released.

Sebastian nearly choked. "What are you...? You can't open a pressurized fuel tank in a vacuum! Can you?"

"I'll let you know."

One year later, on the day the *Eternity* was scheduled to arrive at Terra III, Sebastian held a private memorial for Wild. He had made four catches since the day Wild's Skeeter exploded. The official incident report declared that Wild's docking clamps had malfunctioned, causing his Skeeter to drift away from the colony ship, resulting in spontaneous decompression of his fuel cell. Sebastian had provided key statements in the investigation. Wild would have done the same for him.

That same day, the colonists aboard the *Eternity* were coasting past the outermost orbital of the Terra III system. But Sebastian did not shed any tears for them. It was tough competition out here. If they couldn't take it, they should just move on.

And they did.

Urban Fantasy

You don't need a quest, and elf, or a sword to experience something amazing.

Ten Seconds

Max had the worst malady any middle school kid could have: he was different. Not different in a visible way; teachers at least tried to quash that kind of teasing. They were less proactive about protecting students that could see into the future, even a mere ten seconds.

Ten seconds of precognition was hardly the most useful gift in the world. Max could predict the answers to questions the teacher asked during class, but not on tests. Knowing where the kickball was going didn't keep him from being picked last every time. And being innately difficult to prank only made him a favorite target.

Wednesdays were usually the worst. Fridays he was largely ignored while kids looked forward to their weekend adventures, adventures they recounted to friends in detail the following Mondays. He always dreaded midweek. So it was extra nice that it was a Wednesday that Belinda Johnston joined the class.

Most of the class had finished their spelling homework and Max could hear several boys and even one girl behind him plotting a simultaneous spitwad assault. He knew he was the target. He was always the target. Ten seconds warning was enough to evade a single spitwad, not eight. He was trying to decide if telling the teacher was worth the effort when he realized the door was about to open and the fattest twelve-year-old any of them had ever seen was about to walk in.

The joke wasn't even his idea. Someone else — a girl only a rung above Max on the social ladder — was going to say it and the class was going to laugh and cheer. Cheer for another pariah? Why couldn't they cheer for him? Didn't he deserve, for once in his life, to not feel alone?

"Thar she blows!" Max shouted, stealing the joke.

Everyone looked up in time to see fat Belinda Johnston waddle through the door. Half the fabric of her t-shirt was lost within crevices at her breasts and waistline. Her glasses pinched her face like a red marshmallow in tweezers. She leaned backward. She breathed through her mouth. Everything about this girl begged for harassment.

The class erupted. Max had heard the sound many times, but for once it was the cheers and not the laughs that belonged to him. To his surprise, this felt no better.

The teacher made Max stand in the corner for ten minutes, as if he was a naughty first grader. Ten minutes of secret thumbs ups and nods of approval. It was the most miserable ten minutes of his life. When he was allowed to return to his seat, he found Belinda in the desk beside his.

"Sorry," Max said, not just because the teacher had demanded it.

"No prob," Belinda said. "I knew you were going to say it."

"You did not," Max said. "Ten minutes ago you didn't even know me. Anyone that did know me wouldn't have expected that."

She shrugged. At least Max assumed that's what caused the ripple through her chins. "You were staving off a spitwad attack. I don't blame you." She turned around and handed the boy behind her an open marker. He hadn't asked for it, she just did. The boy seemed as puzzled as Max, but he took it.

"How could you know about the spitwads?" Max said.

"I'm special."

The boy behind Belinda giggled. "Yeah, *speeecial*." He smacked himself in the chest with a limp wrist. He had forgotten the marker in his haste to score the joke and smeared ink all over his shirt with the gesture.

Belinda smiled and took the marker back.

Max did his best to stifle a laugh while the boy wiped vainly at the black marks. He turned back to find Belinda carefully placing three sheets of notebook paper on the floor between their desks.

"It's hard to catch me by surprise," Belinda said. "I'm always ready."

"Not for this bunch." Max knew a kid from the back row was already planning another strike. "You can't always be ready. And these jerks are relentless." Max felt a little ashamed at his sense of relief that Belinda was already becoming the new favorite target.

The teacher turned away and the back row boy made his move. A classic gum-in-hair welcome to the new fat girl. He crouch-ran to her chair, slipped on the paper on the floor and landed on his tailbone.

Max stared at Belinda while the gum boy stood, rubbed his butt, and hobbled back to his seat. "You really knew?"

Belinda winked a pudgy eye. And for the first time in his life, Max did not feel alone.

Glow Baby

Had it really been ten years since I saw this old house? The years must have passed on tiptoes for they had not disturbed a single memory of the property. Stained bricks still peeked past the trellises and vines. The ancient birch still shadowed most of the generous corner lot. I had climbed that tree and played croquet beneath its branches every summer of my childhood. My children were about to have that same chance, assuming fun was to be found in this house of mourning. How would my kids handle watching a man they never knew put into the ground?

Aunt Rose was waiting for us in the driveway. How old she looked! Her brother, my father, had never looked so old, even up until the cancer took him three years ago. He had been very sick those last years, weak, but not old-looking.

From all I'd heard, Rose was in excellent health for a woman of sixty-seven. Yet she looked fifteen years older: the color lost from her hair, cheeks developing jowls, knuckles too large for her hands. She had lost weight in her neck so that folds of skin draped to her collarbone like a tablecloth. But the wide eyes maintained the pale blue kindness I remembered of the Aunt Rosie of my youth.

"Missy," Rose gushed as I opened the car door, "it has been so long. How have you been?" Her voice was tired but bright.

"It's Melissa now, Aunt Rose." I stretched the hours of driving out of my back. "I haven't gone by Missy since high school. Busy is how I've been."

"I can see that." She stooped to look in the window to the backseat. "Get those little ones out here to meet their Great Aunt Rosie. A woman my age can't be kept in suspense like this."

Holly was already climbing out of the car, her chin tucked low in that bashful way she had when she met anyone new. She reluctantly raised her radiant blue eyes to Rose. I gently ushered her forward then bent to retrieve her brother from his car seat.

"You must be Holly," Rose said. "You have your mother's eyes. Has anyone ever told you that?"

Holly nodded.

"Do you have a hug for your Aunt Rosie?"

Holly looked to me questioningly. I hefted Brendan to my hip and nodded reassurance. The hug she delivered wasn't enthusiastic, but it was sincere.

"And who is this big boy?" Rose said, turning toward Brendan and me.

Brendan wriggled to the point I nearly dropped him to the sidewalk. "I Bredan," he said. "I Bredan, I Bredan." I gave up the struggle and let him slide down my leg to the ground. He laughed and ran past the hedge into the yard.

Rose giggled as he passed. "Nice to meet you, Brendan. Make yourself at home."

I gestured for Holly to go watch her brother. "Grant sends his sympathy, but he couldn't get out of work."

"Husbands," Rose said with a shake of the head. "And people wonder why I never had one." We both smiled a moment, then we embraced.

"I hate that it took something like this to get me here," I said into her shoulder. "I'm going to miss him."

"We're all going to miss your grandfather," Rose said. "He is with your father now. We all should be so lucky."

"Were you with Gramps when he—?"

Rose released the hug but maintained a grip on my shoulders. "He passed in his sleep. But enough of that. Your children are even more beautiful than their photos; I can't believe this is the first I've met them. How old are they now?"

"Seven and two."

"It goes so fast." Rose turned as if to watch the children, but her gaze lingered on the house instead. A nervous breath fluttered past her lips before she remembered herself and said, "Come on inside, all of you." Then a smile. "I have someone for you to meet."

Someone to meet? As long as I had known her, Aunt Rose had never introduced anyone. She was the family spinster. Her life never yielded a boyfriend that lasted more than a few months. I always suspected her a virgin; perhaps that was naïve.

"I thought you didn't like suspense, Rosie," I teased. "Who is it?"

"Is it a man?" Holly asked.

I blushed. A fine way for my daughter to emerge from her timidity. But Rose just laughed.

"That would be something, wouldn't it? At my age, would I know what to do with one?"

Rose led us into the living room. Even more than the exterior, the interior was a museum, one perpetual exhibit maintained for generations without end. The red leather chair my father had always loved still squatted in the same corner; the record cabinet still doubled as an end table, complete with the apple-shaped dish I had so often raided for ribbon candy. Even the round coffee table with its absurd, inch-thick protective cushion on top. The whole room was a time capsule.

I dropped my suitcase beside the stairs and looked to Rose. She cleared her throat and shuffled with anticipation, but the room was vacant. If anyone else were in the house, these creaky floorboards would have given them away. The kids both looked at me, sharing my confusion.

Rose lifted a shoebox-size basket from the coffee table and held it close to her face. "Did you miss me, sweetheart," she cooed into the basket. "It's okay, momma's back. You need to meet my niece and her children."

I smiled reluctantly. Holly would be pleased to see a pet in the house. She had spent the last year vowing to be a veterinarian when she grew up. Unfortunately she would have to overcome allergies first. If this was a kitten, we would have to make an immediate trip to the drug store. But the creature inside that basket was definitely not a cat.

The light was the first thing I noticed, the pale halo poking through the gaps in the weaving. The light intensified when Rose reached into the basket. She scooped her hand, her motion cautious and tender. She withdrew the thing and presented it.

It looked like a six-inch, pink bowling pin with arms, or perhaps a chubby stick figure without legs. The arms were rounded nubs reaching aimlessly upward. It had no face, just smooth pink flesh over the entire body. It seemed to have a light bulb inside the way its body glowed. I had seen artificial pets before – robotic dogs, computer programs on keychains

— but I had never seen anything like this.

Rose stroked the wriggling pink thing. "I want you all to meet Cleo."

It was Holly that first mustered some courage. She crept up to Rose, reached out two fingers, and stroked what must have been Cleo's belly. Cleo flapped its stubby arms faster and the glow flickered brighter for an instant.

Holly smiled, looked to Rose's face then mine. "She's warm," Holly said. "And soft like a flower petal."

"She likes you," Rose said.

The question bubbled inside me until I nearly burst. I had to know. "What is it?"

"Not it, she." Rose snuggled it to her cheek. "I grew lonely in this big house all alone. She's a glow baby, the best love money can buy."

"So it's a pet." I moved closer. "Like a robo-pet?"

I nearly cut myself on Rose's glare. "Cleo is no robot." She sheltered the pink lump in her arms. "She is as alive as you or I. And she has more love than any ordinary pet can give. See that light? That's how much Cleo loves me. The more love she gets, the brighter she glows. Better than any tail wag or purr."

A doll that loved her back. That explained it. Gramps was never much on affection. After his stroke, even simple communication became difficult. But Rose stuck in there for years, finally releasing Gramps to hospice care a few weeks before the end. If anyone deserved to be loved back, Rose did.

I made breakfast the next morning, a thank you to Rose for putting us up for the week. The house was not technically hers yet, but it would be once the will was executed. Not only was she the oldest of Gramps' surviving children, she had been his live-in nurse since my grandmother passed away. That had been so long ago, before Holly was born. In all that time I hadn't so much as been to Albany, let alone this house. It felt strange to be back. Or maybe Rose was the strange part.

Holly poured syrup over her pancakes while stealing lingering glances at the glow baby in the basket at Rose's elbow. Its glow seemed subtler now than last night, its motions calmer. For a thing without a face, it seemed happy enough.

Suddenly Holly asked, "How does she eat?"

"Holly, pay attention." I righted the bottle. She had enough syrup for ten pancakes on her two.

"Cleo doesn't need to eat." Rose tickled Cleo under what passed as its chin. "Like John Lennon, all she needs is love."

"So where do these glow babies come from, Aunt Rosie," I asked. She insisted it was alive, but who ever heard of an animal that did not eat? "Is it like some sort of special cactus?"

"She is not a plant." Impatience dripped from her words like the syrup from Holly's fork. "Cleo may not be human, but she is my baby. Do people interrogate dog owners like this?"

"I didn't mean—" But I did mean it. This pink mass was not a real…anything. I decided to redirect. "Where did you find her?"

"There is a kiosk at Colonie Mall selling them. They are the latest thing. That horrible socialite that is always on the news, she has one. So does the anchorwoman on channel six. And that actress from the plane movie."

"But what's the source? Some island somewhere?"

"Oh, that's a secret. Did the Colonel ever reveal his recipe?" She picked up Cleo and cradled it to her bosom. "It doesn't matter where she came from. She belongs here with me."

"I like her," Holly said through her napkin. "I like the way she wiggles."

"Do you want to hold her?"

Holly's fork clattered. The twinkle that danced in my daughter's eye told me how cruel it would be to protest. Rose passed the pink pet gently into Holly's little hands. The creature's light wavered. Holly tucked it close to her neck and stroked its back. It brightened. So did Holly's face.

"Mom, did you see that? I made her happy. I think she likes me."

Rose stood beside Holly's chair. "Of course she likes you. Glow babies love visiting with new people, but they are happiest with their mamas." Rose leaned down and touched her nose to Cleo's tiny pink head, creating a kind of three-way cuddle. Cleo's limbs twitched with what could have been excitement or horror. The light was now so bright I had to look away. That was when I realized Brendan had left the table.

A brief search of the downstairs found him playing with his dinosaurs in the old den. It was the one room in the whole house I did not recognize. The wood paneling was still there, the black floor tiles, the little half bath with the curtain-door, but the furniture I remembered was gone. There used to be two long cushions that passed as couches, one along each side wall with lamps above that made for perfect reading. Now there was a table full of medicine vials, a small stash of oxygen tanks, and a hospital-style adjustable bed. Brendan's stegosaurus was defending the bed's elevated footrest from an improbable allosaurus-triceratops alliance.

"Brendan, sweetheart, you need to take your dinosaurs somewhere else."

The steg roared and tail swiped the allosaur off the bed, clanking against the oxygen. He grabbed a brontosaurus from a sack on the floor to take its place.

"Brendan Michael Harlan, I mean it! This room is not for playing." Not anymore. I snatched the dino-sack from the floor beside him.

He abandoned his active toys in favor of the sack. "No! That's mine!"

I dropped the sack on the kitchen floor. He scrambled for it while I cleared the room of the rest of his toys. Another coaxing hand sent him jabbering toward the living room.

Alone in the den, I approached the bed but could not bear to touch it. There I stood, thinking of all the old experiences I shared with my grandfather...and the recent ones I had not. I was his first granddaughter and he always treated me special.

"You know he didn't die there."

I flinched. Rose had appeared beside me, that luminous pink cherub dangling at her bosom from a sling around her neck. Its light cast an eerily bloody tint on the bed sheets.

"He was such a proud man when I knew him," I whispered. "It's hard to imagine him like that...in this bed."

Rose straightened the sheets where Brendan had ruffled them. There was an efficient precision to her motion. "I need not imagine, only remember."

The funeral director turned out to be an old family friend. He dropped by the house the next day to share his condolences and iron out some details for both the wake and burial. In two days there would be a requiem mass followed by the long trip to the cemetery. But first we had to get through tomorrow's viewing — greeting all those old friends from lives long past, many of whom no one would remember, save perhaps Rose.

How many would attend that missed Daddy's funeral? No one had expected long-lost friends to travel hundreds of miles to bury someone they had neither seen nor thought of in decades. So Dad's funeral in Charlotte had been a quiet affair with only new friends in attendance. This would be quite different.

Aunt Linda came by the house to participate in the planning. She was the youngest of my father's siblings, less than a decade my senior. She had always been more like a cousin than an aunt, more comfortable to talk with. Her input was minimal, mostly trivial cosmetic details Gramps never would have noticed or cared about. She did find opportunity to flash an unpleasant frown at Brendan when he escaped his older sister's supervision long enough to flap through our discussion with his pterodactyl wings. The mortician cracked a smile without dropping a syllable of his diatribe on the duties of pallbearers.

Through all of this — funeral planning, pterodactyl invasions, and all — Rose sat in her floral chair rocking little Cleo like a colicky baby. Hers was the primary voice of reason in the plans, always knowing what Gramps would want, always concise in her requests. No flowers inside the casket. The biggest display should rest against Grandmother's headstone, not his. Only family should be pallbearers. No singing in Latin. Not once did she mention Cleo to anyone, but neither did she try to hide the luminous presence. The pink elephant in the room was simply not discussed.

When the meeting ended, Rose walked the director to his car and I seized the opportunity to ask Linda about Rose's new accessory.

"Oh, isn't it the cutest?" Linda replied. "I saw one on one of those morning shows the other day. They are just so precious. Course, Dad didn't much care for that one."

"When did Gramps see Cleo?"

Linda looked down her substantial nose in what I remember Gramps calling her gossip gaze. "It was a few weeks before Dad went to hospice that Rose got it." Linda chanced a look out the window before continuing. "The two never did get along. Its little light dimmed every time they were in the same room. Didn't do Dad's glow no good, either."

"So you were here when Gramps and that thing were together?"

"Once," Linda said, leaning closer, "but not here."

"She brought it to the hospice?"

"Rose brings Cleo everywhere. Toward the end, Dad refused to see Rose if Cleo was with her, least the times he was coherent enough to decide. Even in his bad spells, he knew he didn't like her none."

"Why did Gramps dislike it so much?"

The front door opened. Cleo seemed dimmer than before. Rose stroked its bulb of a hand as she looked from Linda to me and back again. "Second thoughts on the casket?" Rose asked. She knew we were talking about her.

"Or was it the flowers?"

"We were talking about Cleo," I confessed.

Linda's mouth fell open. The women in her family simply did not express truths to each other that way. Fortunately the men had been raised differently, and Daddy had passed his candor on to me.

"About Cleo?"

"About Gramps and Cleo," I said.

"There were plenty of people Father did not appreciate in life," Rose said. "More than a few. Some of those will undoubtedly be paying their respects tomorrow, just as Father did to the ones he outlived."

Linda gathered her purse. "Rose, be reasonable."

Rose puckered her lips. "And you two are the arbiters of reason?"

"Aunt Rosie, you just told the funeral director everything your father wanted to happen at his funeral. Everything. You knew the songs he wanted, the prayers, what to dress him in. In your heart, does he want Cleo there?"

Rose continued stroking Cleo's nub. The air was stale with pink-tinted silence. Linda was the first to exit the extinct conversation. I went to find the kids soon after. Rose was still standing in the kitchen when I passed with a soiled Brendan in tow. By the time I finished changing him, both she and her car were gone.

Holly was the first to hear the car return to the driveway. "Aunt Rosie is back." She clapped her hands and ran to the back door. She had no knowledge of the kitchen argument and was excited at her great aunt's return. At least one of us was. Brendan followed his sister to the kitchen.

"Young lady, get your brother away from those stairs." The tiny mudroom between the kitchen and back door also opened to the basement stairwell. I fell down those stairs when I was eleven and preferred my children not share the experience. I had to wrestle them both away from the mudroom and hold them for a good two minutes. When the door finally opened, Holly squealed.

"You got it!" That excitement had not inhabited her voice in years. "I can't believe you really got it. Mom, she got it!"

"Apparently. Aunt Rosie, what did you get that has my daughter so—" Then I saw the box. Despite its size and shape, I knew its contents were not shoes. The soft light that emanated from the open top was not pink but green.

Rose brushed past me to Holly. "I told you I would. I know you will take good care of him."

"It's a boy?" Holly asked through tears.

Rose laughed. "What do you think?" She lowered the box for all to see.

It didn't look exactly like Cleo. This green one was shorter with slightly different proportions: smaller head, larger waist, reminiscent of an overturned brandy snifter. Its illumination was evident, but nowhere near as brilliant as Cleo's shine. Holly lifted it out of the box with quivering hands. The light grew just enough to be noticeable.

I pulled Rose back into the mudroom by the elbow. "Rosie! Do you really think she is ready for that kind of responsibility? She's only seven."

"What responsibility? No feeding, no mess, no noise. A glow baby is the perfect pet. He needs nothing from Holly but love." She nudged me back through the doorway. Holly was waltzing through the kitchen with her little green man. "Do you think she can handle that?"

No smile had so completely conquered my daughter's face since she was Brendan's age. Pure elation. Could I deny my daughter that? I continued to debate myself despite the certainty of surrender. "It can't come to the wake," I said. It was as close to a yes as I could muster.

Holly squeaked. "So I can keep him? Really keep him?"

Rose was chuckling again. "And your mother is right about the funeral home. That is no place for so delicate a creature as a glow baby."

I raised an eyebrow. "Isn't it?"

Rose sighed. "It is not." She poked Cleo in the belly like the Pillsbury Dough Boy. Her hand was shaking. "Cleo will be all right for a few hours. I will leave her here in her favorite basket with—" she leaned past me and called to Holly. "So what is the little guy's name going to be?"

Holly's forehead wrinkled in concentration. "What was Great Gramp's name?"

Rose smiled wanly. "Oscar."

Holly nodded. "Then I'll call him that. Oscar."

What would Gramps think of that tribute?

It was five hours and twenty-seven minutes that we were away from the house. The line of condolences was never-ending and the sentiments shared were endearing. Even Rose was swept up in the loving atmosphere. She wore no watch and asked no one for the time until the very last of Gramps' old friends had paid his respects. She even did a fair job of containing her anxiety through the ride home.

The car door was open before we came to a complete stop. She was a sight, the sixty-seven year old scuffling up the sidewalk like a fretful toddler in heels. She took the back stairs by twos and was inside the house before I had Brendan free from his restraints. The spectacle had me giggling all the way to the back door.

Then I heard the scream.

Rose stood in the dark living room, leaning over the small padded hamper. None of the lamps were lit, the only illumination coming through the front window or through the doorway behind me. No light emanated from the basket.

Rose reached for the basket's tiny occupant but could not convince her trembling hands to touch it. She finally collapsed, sobbing into the basket. Her gasps were guttural, wheezing, hopeless. It was as I stood there, watching my altruistic aunt weep, that I realized the tears she shed for her faceless pet were the first I had seen from her all day. She had not cried on anyone's shoulder, dropped not one tear over her father's open casket. In spite of myself, my pity turned to ire.

Holly pushed past me into the room, saw her aunt, and raced up the stairs. "Oscar," I heard her relieved little voice flutter in the distance, "you're okay!" I sighed in relief for my daughter. To my surprise, Rose shared my sigh. Her weeping stopped suddenly and she pulled her face out of the basket. She was flushed.

No, it was too dark in the room to see that kind of detail. The rosiness on her cheeks was not her own.

Brendan kicked, stirring my senses. I had forgotten I was holding him. I set him down and approached Rose, placed my hand on her back. She shrugged me away.

"Aunt Rosie," I whispered, "it—she's all right?"

"I don't know." She pulled Cleo from the basket. "I don't know if you killed her or not."

"Killed her? Rose, that's insane."

"Is it? You took me away from her for hours." She brandished the limp doll as if it were a crucifix and I a vampire. "Five hours. You and that old man hate her, want to destroy her, want to take everything from me."

"Old man?" The heat grew in my face. "Gramps is dead; your *father* is dead. You care more about that damn doll than—"

"Get away from me." She clutched Cleo to her shoulder as she sidestepped past me toward the kitchen. "Stay away from us." She shouted more, but it was unintelligible. The babbling continued as she crossed the checkerboard floor and locked herself in the room with the oxygen tanks.

The next morning came and went and the den door did not open. "Come on, Rose, we'll to be late for mass."

No answer. Not a sound passed through the door, the same door I had pressed my ear to as a child to listen to grownups talking about Christmas presents. I had never encountered another door so flimsy, but still no sound could be heard within. Scenarios started to unravel in my head.

"Aunt Rose, are you okay?" I hammered the door. "Rosie, it's time to go."

I ransacked the table beside Rose's floral chair and found the ring of house keys Grandmother had always kept in the back. Still there after all these years. The third one worked and I flung the den door wide.

Rose was lying in the adjustable bed, legs and head raised, cradling Cleo like a new mother in a maternity ward. Her hair was matted, her eyes puffy with exhaustion. Cleo glowed like a cool ember, not brilliant but consistent.

"Aunt Rose?"

"She is still weak," Rose said shakily. "She needs me."

"She looks fine. Cleo is better; you nursed her through it."

Rose shook her head.

"Bring her with you. It will be fine, but we have to—"

"Go without me," Rose mumbled.

She was right; I had to go. Rose was a mess. Either she missed the mass or we all missed it. I had not driven hundreds of miles to babysit a sixty-seven year old woman.

The kids tromped down the stairs. I didn't want them to see Rose this way. "Fine," I said as evenly as my voice could manage, "skip the mass. Pull yourself together. Just make sure you're at the cemetery by two. I will make excuses for you the best I can." I closed the door and we left.

It was a quarter to five when I burst through the den door. Gramps was in the ground and no one had seen Rose. She was right where I had left her, only her hair was done, she seemed to have showered, and she wore a red sundress.

I somehow suppressed the urge to slap her. "He was your father."

"Shh, you'll disturb Cleo."

"Your father! He might not have shown it, but everyone knew he loved you best. The daughter he loved best could not be bothered to attend his funeral."

"I had to take care of Cleo."

I pushed my fingers through my hair, wanting desperately to jerk it out by the roots and throw it at her. "You took care of him for years. How could you not go to the funeral?"

"Some things are more important."

"More important than saying goodbye?" I kicked the table. A symphony of vials plinked to the floor. "Nothing is that important."

"Love is that important."

"It's a damn doll! A doll over your father?"

"Cleo loves me. She needed me." Her expression remained calm. She did not raise her voice, not so much as a tense muscle. Somehow Rose was at peace with her absence.

"Gramps needed you there. We needed you."

"Your grandfather is dead. Cleo is not."

"Not dead? Cleo was never alive!"

"Why would you say such a thing?"

"Let's see…it doesn't eat or sleep or breathe or do anything. That is a toy. If you thought otherwise, you were scammed."

Rose's calm smile faded to an expression of Zen serenity. "Is that what alive is? You wanted me at a funeral for my dead father and *that* is your definition of life?" She shook her head.

I tried to scream at her, to defy her warped logic. I was out of words but not out of anger, so I stomped up to the guestroom and slammed the door, twice. I lay on the three-quarter-size bed and seethed at the ceiling.

It was after midnight when I jolted awake, still in my funeral garb, still deeply hurt by Rose's betrayal of my grandfather. It was a sound that stirred me, a high-pitched weeping. I rubbed my eyes and stepped into the hall. The cries came from the bathroom. I tapped on the door. It creaked open.

Holly was sitting on the toilet with all her clothes on and the lights off. Her hair curtained her face. The room was bathed in dim green light. Oscar wriggled in her lap.

She looked up just long enough to recognize me. "Go away. It's my fault, just go away."

"What's your fault, sweetheart?"

She lifted her glow baby. "Just look at him. He hardly wiggles, he's getting darker."

"It's plenty bright, sweetheart. Let's go back to bed." I took her hand.

She brushed me away. "No, no. Not until Oscar is better. Not until he's bright."

"You can make him brighter tomorrow."

"You don't get it. If I don't get him brighter, he might go out. Aunt Rose said so, he needs my love. He needs it now. I'll never let you go out, Oscar, no matter what it costs."

The rest was a blur. I loaded the suitcases with whatever was already inside them. I carried a sleeping Brendan to the car, then came back for Holly. I carried her with one arm and wrestled ferociously for the green monster with the other. We were at the back door before I pried it from her fingers.

She slapped me.

Never before had my daughter struck me, not with malice. I hesitated in the tiny mudroom; furious, delirious, witless. The doll writhed in my fingers as if fighting to escape my grip. I extended my arm toward the basement stairs and granted its wish.

Holly's cries were deafening.

Oscar bounced off the top step, then the third, the fifth. I was out the door before the damned thing struck the basement floor. I thrust my hysterical daughter into the car, waking Brendan who added to the wails. A moment later we were out of the drive.

As we drove away, I am sure I saw two lights — one pink and one green — dancing in the den window.

Faerie Belches

I never used to hear them. No matter how quiet the setting – the back corner of the library, taking out the trash on a still night, lying in bed wishing for sleep – the sound never found me. Now I hear them everywhere. They're such tiny little pops other people don't seem to notice, the way you sometimes notice a television is on even when the screen is blank. It could be the sound of a soap bubble bursting or a butterfly sneeze, but it isn't. It's faerie belches.

I stopped believing in faeries long before I'd ever heard one belch. I hadn't even clapped for Tinkerbelle on my third grade trip to the theater. It took someone like Krystal to wake me to their mischievous emissions. Krystal, another creature whose existence I hadn't noticed.

"Did you hear that?" Those were the first words she ever said to me. At least the first words I remember. I was chasing a foul kickball into her lonely corner of the schoolyard on a lovely spring Monday. Did I hear that? I hadn't heard anything, so I pretended not to hear her either. That was the way our whole fifth-grade class treated her and I was right with them. Don't hear her, don't talk to her, don't even see her. What kind of kid dressed like that? Always with a black t-shirt under an oversized brown or olive unbuttoned shirt, a necktie slung loose to her collarbone, and enough eyeliner to warrant the nickname Raccoon Girl. It wasn't like she was some rocker rebel; she did her homework, kept her hands in her pockets, and never made eye contact with anyone over two feet tall. She was weird, which in fifth grade made her a leper. Even in her empty corner of the schoolyard where I was chasing a foul kickball, the answer was no, I didn't hear anything. I simply grabbed the ball and tromped back to the game.

"You will," she said behind me.

* * *

It was later that same night I heard it the first time. I was up late, finishing a book report I'd ignored for a month and was due tomorrow. It seemed to happen every time I hit the period. It was a tiny little sound, imperceptible but unignorable.

Pp.

At first I thought I'd spilled on the keyboard, the sound of a droplet of cola delaying the key for a millisecond, but the sound persisted even after the printed pages were securely in their plastic cover. *Pp.* When I was got in bed. *Pp.* As I got out of the shower the next morning. Pp, *Pp.* They were even distracting me at school during tests. *Pp.*

"They're faerie burps," Krystal told me after school on Thursday. She and I both had to wait a long time for our rides on Thursdays. My mom volunteered at the library that day. I'm not sure what her mom did. Anyway, it was the first she'd spoken to me since the playground.

"Sorry?" I looked around as if I didn't know who was talking. I was actually checking to see who might overhear us. My rep couldn't handle a hit like talking to Raccoon Girl.

"I saw you look up during the spelling test. You heard them, too, didn't you. The faeries."

I delayed my response too long. I should have told her I heard nothing and not to talk to me. Instead I just stood there dumbly and wished for an excuse to leave.

Pp.

I flinched, glanced over my shoulder as if someone was there. There was nothing. There never was. I looked back to see her smiling at the ground. "I knew you did." Then my mom pulled up and I was saved from having to reply. I heard the tiny belches all the way home.

A month went by and they became more and more frequent. *Pp* during classes. *Pp* when I watched TV. Even in the lunchroom, *Pp, Pp, Pp.* I was getting desperate, so I finally did it. It was the first time the cafeteria seat beside her wasn't empty; my butt filled it. "How do I make them stop?" I demanded and tossed a grape nervously into my mouth.

Krystal continued to stare into the pudding cup she always brought but never ate. "You can't. Faeries burp a lot and no one notices. But me. And now you. You get used to them."

"I don't want to get used to them. I want them to stop."

"No you don't. Hearing them makes you special. Don't you want to be special?"

"Not your kind of special," I said without thinking. She didn't have time to take offense.

"Mikey and 'Coon Girl sittin' in a tree…,'" began the chant from down the table. It didn't last long; a cafeteria monitor silenced them, but just its beginning was enough to mark my plummet into loserdom. I wouldn't be playing kickball tomorrow, fat Francis would be picked instead. I wouldn't be helping Trevor and Hannah pass love notes to each other in science class; they'd pass it around me or use the pencil sharpener diversion. My social standing was now low enough to be jeered. I was a loser, or would be unless I did something fast to counteract the chant.

It was low of me, I admit. Even then I knew how low it was, but it was all I could think of. I had to turn the focus of ridicule solely onto Raccoon Girl, which meant making her look really stupid and make it clear it was my fault. I thought up the dirtiest names I could call her, took a deep breath…*Pp*…and choked on a grape.

No sound came out of my mouth because no air did. I couldn't breathe! I stumbled to my feet and tried in vain to cough. My eyes bulged, pleading for someone to help me. The monitor had already walked away. Trevor and Hannah just stared at me as if I was a curious but unentertaining television commercial, faces stagnant and emotionless. The rest of the class shared their bemusement. The entire cafeteria seemed eerily still; all but Krystal.

She had her arms around me before I knew she was behind me. I felt the thumb side of her fist nestle my belly, then a squeeze. *Pp*. The grape flew across the table and hit Trevor in the eye. Cool, grease-flavored air gushed into me. My knees buckled and Krystal helped me back to my seat.

A few kids understood what had happened and started to clap. The sound spread like a juicy rumor and soon the entire cafeteria was applauding the girl with the eye liner and necktie. Her face was already back in her pudding cup.

That Thursday we found ourselves waiting for our rides again. "I'm sorry," she said when she caught me glancing at her.

I was taken aback. "Thank you," I said. "For the Hemlock Maneuver, not the apology. What are you sorry about, saving my life?"

"It's Heimlich Maneuver, and no." She actually looked me in the eye for the first time. "I'm sorry I made you choke."

I barely heard the words under the spell of her stare. Those outlined eyes were glorious. Brilliant green with rusty flecks of brown scattered trough them. I'd never noticed any girl's eyes that much before, certainly not the color. I was transfixed in her intoxicating gaze.

She looked away and I could speak again. "You didn't make me choke, I choked on a grape. You got it out, not in."

"I knew you were going to say something horrible." Her eyes were on her own toes. I longed for them to find me again. "So I wished something would stop you. And it did."

"Coincidence," I said. "Like the time I wished my mother would show up, just as she turned the corner. Or yesterday when I wished Ms. Fields wouldn't give us the science test, and her copy machine turned out broke. Things like that happen."

"Things like that happen when you hear faerie burps."

"What?"

Her eyes were closed now, face still angled toward her shoes. "If you make a wish and hear a faerie burp at the same time, it comes true. But it has to be the same time or it doesn't count." I was only half listening, instead trying to see her eyes, still wishing she would raise them to me.

Pp.

And she was looking at me. Then my mom pulled into the parking lot. Maybe Krystal had wished for it that time. I hadn't.

From then on, Francis had my spot in every kickball game. He couldn't catch and never kicked the ball in the air, but he played. I didn't even think about wishing him back out. My rep never recovered from that day in the cafeteria. I knew I could hang with the cooler kids again if I wanted, if I wished it, but it wasn't worth what I'd be giving up. I never heard a *Pp* in the middle of a kickball game. Or passing love notes. Or picking on a less cool kid. And no cool kid ever looked at me the way Krystal did.

I'd love to tell you Krystal and I ended up dating through junior high. I'd love to tell you we became the best of friends. We didn't. She moved away a couple weeks into sixth grade. I never seemed to time that wish quite right. Now I have but one wish left: that she might read this story and know I miss her. *Pp.*

Excuse Me

"So tell me, Mr. Flugle," Dr. Kwack said in his best over-the-top Freudian impression, "vhat zeems to be the problem?"

"Please," I said from the vinyl chaise, "call me Gary." I never liked my last name. Flugle is such a silly sounding name. Dr. Kwack probably hadn't noticed.

"Very well, Gary it is. What's the problem Gary? Is it a mother issue?" Did I mention Freud?

"No," I said reflexively. "It's more complex than that."

"A father issue?"

"No."

"It's sex then."

"Um…no, it's not sex."

"It's all right," he lulled, his phony accent wavering. "Many people have sex issues."

"It's not sex," I assured him. "Like I said, it's complex."

He thought on this for a moment. "Sex with your mother?"

"Leave my mother out of this!"

"So it is a mother issue."

I sat up. "I already told you it's not anything like that. It's…"

"Complex," Kwack finished with me. "So it's sex with your…"

"Would you let me tell you?" My eyes scoured the wall in search of his license. I was curious whether it came from a cereal box or a happy meal.

Kwack couldn't handle the hiatus. "Is it your sister?"

"Every time I fart, I travel back in time seven seconds." There was a moment of silence while the insanity of my words filled the room. "Doctor?"

"Back in time you say?"

"Yes."

"When you do what?"

"When I fart."

"As in…?"

"As in pass gas."

"I see."

"Break wind. Release flatulence. Poot. Cut the…"

"I said I see." There was another moment, this one more a moment of twitchiness than silence, but the twitching was noiseless. "And what makes you so sure you travel back in time when you do this?"

"I live the seven seconds preceding a release twice, once before and once right after."

"A release?"

"A fart. Keep up man, you're the doctor."

"Am I?" Kwack glanced about the room and decided I was probably right. "Why seven seconds?"

"I don't know."

"Why not a minute or a week or something like that?"

"I said I don't know. Why does it happen when I fart?"

"Another good question," said Kwack, seeming impressed.

"I mean why not when I burp or sneeze or have an orgasm?"

"Ooh, that last one would be nice, wouldn't it?"

"But it only happens when I fart."

"When did you start having this delusion, Gary?"

"Which delusion?"

"The time travel delusion."

"It's not a delusion."

"Then why did you come to a psychiatrist?"

I sighed. "Honestly, I have a hard time dealing with the whole thing. Plus I found a coupon in the paper."

"Ah you have a coupon. Excellent. You can pick up your free snow cone maker on the way out."

"Okay."

"It's a very good snow cone maker, you know. Not one of those cheap ones they sell in toy stores."

"Like I was saying, I have trouble dealing with it."

"What's to have trouble with? You just put the ice in the top and it comes out a snow cone. You have to put on the flavor yourself, but that's no harder than pouring something onto another something."

"No, not the snow cone maker."

"So you'd rather have the toaster?"

"I'd rather talk about my problem."

"With the toaster?"

"With my time traveling farts!"

Kwack blinked twice. "Of course, the delusion."

"Would you stop calling it that?" I was screaming now, as I suspect you deduced on your own. "When I fart, I travel back in time. It really happens; it's not a delusion. I just need some help coping with the issues that stem from inadvertent time travel, specifically time travel that begins and ends with the same expulsion of gas from my anus."

"When you put it that way it all sounds perfectly sane. So tell me, Gary, when did you first notice that your farts made you travel back in time?"

"I guess that would be when I was a child. About three. It's one of my earliest memories. That and my father backing over the cat with the Winnebago."

"Aha, so it is a father issue. I knew it."

"My father?" I repeated much as one would if told his father was responsible for something as preposterous as time traveling flatulence. "No, my father only backed over Eddie."

"And who was Eddie?"

"The cat."

"What cat?"

"The cat my father backed over with the Winnebago."

"Aha, so it is a father issue."

"Are you even listening?"

Kwack lowered the legal pad he was supposedly using for notes. "I'm sorry, what was that?"

"I was trying to tell you how I first discovered my problem."

"Right, your father problem."

"Whatever. I was learning to use proper manners at the time. You know, say 'please' when you want something, 'thank you' when you get it, 'sorry' when you break it, and of course don't say anything at all if adults are talking, even though they forget to say please or thank you and never say they're sorry regardless of who broke what."

"What's an eight letter word for domination starting with H?"

"Hegemony, why?"

Kwack glared at his notes for a moment, nodded agreeably, scribbled something down, then stared at me as if he expected me to speak. I looked at him similarly. The expectancy built until we both lost track of what we were expecting.

"Weren't you saying something about manners?" Kwack asked finally.

"Right," I said, since for once he was. "I discovered it when my mother was teaching me to say 'excuse me' when I'd do something impolite—I swear, if you say this is a mother issue I'm going to jam that pencil into your temple."

Kwack slowly lowered his finger which was already in position to punctuate the "Aha!" that was about to leap from his mouth.

"I handled the burps all right," I continued. "I would release a little frog-croak, say 'excuse me', and all would be forgiven. I never got punished when I burped. My farts, on the other hand, landed me in a world of trouble."

"You said it too early."

"Said what too early?"

"Excuse me."

"You're excused, Doctor."

"No, you twit, you got in trouble because you said 'excuse me' too early."

"Did you just call me a twit?"

"Relax. You're in therapy."

"I'll need therapy after this session."

"One session isn't enough to fix your problem."

"How do you know? I haven't finished explaining my problem."

"Have you started?"

"Of course I've started. And yes, I got in trouble for saying 'excuse me' before I farted instead of after. At least that's how my mother—don't forget the pencil—perceived it. From her perspective it would go: 'excuse me'—sound similar to a distressed duck—horrible smell. Often followed by foul language and a spanking—the threat holds double if you touch that one. But I was certain the sequence went distressed duck—'excuse me'—horrible smell. But it was still followed by the language and the spanking."

"And which sequence do you believe?"

I sighed. "Neither, really. To an observer outside our space-time continuum, the sequence would probably be: distressed duck—time warp—'excuse me'—duck catches up, still in a fair amount of distress — horrible smell."

"I disagree," Kwack added as if he were actually listening. "I think, to someone outside our space-time continuum, the event would look like the changing room at a lingerie shop."

"Why would my fart and time travel look like a lingerie shop."

"The changing room in a lingerie shop."

"Why that?"

"I know if I could step outside our space-time continuum and watch you fart, I wouldn't; I'd go peep into the changing rooms of a lingerie shop. As would most men. And some women. I should know, I'm a psychologist."

"Psychiatrist."

"Whatever." Kwack shrugged. "Listen, I have a solution for you. Count."

"Oh, I'm not a count. I have an aunt that insists she's the Duchess of Wisconsin, but…"

"No, count. With numbers."

"One, two, three, four, five, six, seven, eight, nine, ten, eleven, twelve, thir…"

"Not now. Count when you fart. If it's seven seconds you travel back, count to seven then say excuse me."

"You let me count all the way to twelve and a half before telling me what you meant? Are you just trying to fill time in this session?"

"I'm trying to find a nine letter word for euphemism. No wait, I was trying to help you."

"Euphemism is nine letters. And you haven't helped me a bit."

"Sure I did. With the counting thing. I'm not as bad at this as you think I am."

"You couldn't be."

"Sorry?"

"Not as sorry as I am, Doc. At least that bell means we're out of time."

Kwack did a double take. "The timer didn't ring."

"…five, six, seven." *Ding!* "Like I said, time's up Doc. And enjoy that one; it was a stinker."

Near Future SF

Just because it hasn't happened yet doesn't mean it won't happen tomorrow.

Scott W. Baker

How Quickly We Forget

Jack Spiegel burst into the lobby of Lobe Industries, two Keystone rent-a-cops tripping along behind him. He was at the front desk before anyone realized what was happening. "Who the hell do I have to talk to to get some damn answers?"

This was my cue. I introduced myself as Michael Jordan, CEO of Lobe. Speigel didn't blink. Bad sign.

"I don't know what kind of scam you're running, Jordan," Speigel shouted, "but I'll be damned if I'm going to pay a red dime to you, I don't care how many lawyers or collection agents or bounty hunters or whatever the hell you send to my house. I am not an idiot."

"You have a question about the bill?"

"I shouldn't have a damn bill. I don't even know what the hell you're selling. I sure as hell didn't buy any of it. Shove your bill up your — "

"Mr. Spiegel, please, there is no reason to resort to such language." I ushered him into the small office we reserved for dissatisfied clients. "I am certain we can work this out."

Spiegel entered the office timidly, a complete reversal from the body language he entered with. "How... how do you know my name?"

I dismissed the worthless guards and helped Spiegel into his seat. "We have been sending you bills, obviously we know who you are."

"Have we met?" he asked.

I nodded. "More than once."

Spiegel grunted in disbelief. "I usually never forget a face."

"So you told us when we first met. That memory was the reason you came to us."

Spiegel scratched his head; his hand lingered as if wondering where the rest of his hair had gone. He was deteriorating quickly. This was going to be quick and unpleasant.

"Didn't you hear a word I said?" He was exasperated. Who could blame him? "I didn't come to you for anything."

"Then how did you know where to find our office?"

The look on Spiegel's face told the whole story. He tried to answer anyway. "The return address on the bill?"

"A post office box." I moved to the seat next to him, like a friend. "Jack, you came to us a week ago about your daughter, Helen."

"Daughter? I don't have a daughter. I'm telling you, you've got the wrong guy."

"You're Jack Spiegel of Michigan Lane, Baltimore. You run a textiles company that operates out of Juarez. Your cat's name is Rover, your mother's maiden name is Grant." His eyes were wide. He remembered all of this. Lucky.

"And Jack," I continued, "you came to us to remove the memory of your daughter. You paid us thirteen thousand up front with an equal balance to be paid after the procedure was complete. We have obviously removed the memory, but you haven't paid the balance."

"But I didn't — "

"If you remembered coming to us, you would know there was something you forgot. It is standard procedure to erase the visit as well."

Spiegel laughed nervously. "Next you're going to tell me I'm a double agent from Mars."

"Mr. Spiegel, please."

"Why would I want to forget my own daughter?" His eyes widened. He turned his head in slow motion. "She's dead, isn't she?" Was he remembering or figuring it out?

"I'm sorry," was all I said.

"Did I kill her somehow?"

"There was a collision, but you were not in the car. It was a cab. You were late picking her up at the airport. You blamed yourself."

Spiegel wept into his own hand. I let him cry a moment before placing my hand on his shoulder. He tried to embrace me. I resisted. Sometimes that's the hardest part of the job, not hugging a grown man in tears. I never would have believed it.

"If I wanted to forget, why are you telling me?"

"We eradicated those pathways in the brain. You will not remember a word of it once you leave this office." It was technically true.

"I...I'm sorry," he said. He was better at pulling himself together than most. "You're just doing what I hired you for. Forgive me, Mister..."

"Clooney," I finished for him. "George Clooney. I'm your case worker."

"Right."

"I'm afraid I need the balance of that payment now, Mr. Spiegel."

"Of course." He pulled out his checkbook. "Who do I make this out to?"

"Just 'Lobe' is fine. Thirteen thousand."

He repeated as he wrote. "Thirteen... thousand... to... Lobe. Is that you? Lobe?"

"No sir. Lobe is the name of the company. My name is Abraham Lincoln. Doctor Abraham Lincoln."

Spiegel nodded slowly. "Right, that sounds familiar. And you performed the... what was it again?"

"We just call it a procedure. Your signature on the check?"

"Right." They always say that a lot toward the end. "Jack Spiegel. How do you spell that?"

I recited the letters for him as he scrawled. He removed the check slowly, like an elderly woman at the supermarket. He folded it in half, retracing the crease three times before handing it over. I snatched it from his fingers just as the first drool started to collect at the corner of his mouth. Then I hit the buzzer.

The Keystone twins were quick to arrive. I pointed to Spiegel. "He'll be broccoli in an hour. Get him in an ambulance."

"Right away, Mr. Kilburn."

As soon as they were clear I dialed Adams, the VP of accounting. "The Spiegel account is closed," I told him.

"Excellent," Adams said. "I'll make sure legal has his file ready for the lawsuit. Seven waivers; I'm not sure why they bother anymore."

"I'm just glad we got paid, sir. Another five minutes, he wouldn't have known the pen from a popsicle."

"Ninety-three percent success rate and Congress still makes us collect a week later. Pesky slow-degraders would have us out of business without people like you."

I smiled. "Try not to forget that."

Secondhand Rush

Who could blame them? With their minds forever locked in that box, they were bound to grow insufferably bored. Nothing to see, to hear, to feel; nothing but memories of a fleshtime long surrendered for immortality. How long could one's own memories be sufficient? A year? A decade? Eventually they needed fresh memories, someone else's memories.

Their need was my passport to that world, a world of unending life, devoid of fear and pain and frailty. A world without Multiple Sclerosis. They lived in a world I wanted, and I had the memories they craved in spades.

Yet there was prohibitive expense associated with entering the box. With the storage block, consciousness modules, eternal shelf rental for hardware, and of course the cerebral scan and body disposal, the price of transferral could easily run eight digits. One could dedicate a fleshtime to acquiring the funds for transfer, pitting savings against nature in a race to dictate eternity.

But not me.

I typically scraped just enough cash to sustain my body on pizza, tequila, and prescriptions. The dollar was not the currency of my future. Money was meaningless inside the box. Most of them had money, to be sure, but Boxies didn't buy food or houses or cosmetic surgery or Turtle Wax. All they needed was entertainment. Memories. The more exciting and exotic the memory, the more outside-money they would pay to get it. Of course, I wouldn't see a dime until I was ready for transfer.

My tibia had just shed the cast from my most recent exploit: instigating a stampede of Angus cattle and riding the wave of beef like a 1970's surf bum. Experiences like that were marketable for their uniqueness, broken limbs and all. How many people — in or out of the box — could claim to have surfed livestock? Or done a handstand on a moving roller coaster? Or broken three limbs and dislocated a hip jumping down an elevator shaft (a stunt that didn't go as planned, but still a worthy memory)?

Unfortunately the cattle wave had exhausted my personal creativity. I needed a golden carrot; all I could dig up were small potatoes. Rather than sit and think of my own carrot, I went in search of someone else's. The nets were teeming with specific requests the Boxies would pay to acquire.

The high end of the list was jammed with dozens of duplicate results, all requests for death. The death memory was the Boxies' grail. They all wanted it eventually and the going rate was fifteen million. D-15 they called it. I knew of people who tried to deliver a D-15. Not one collected.

Dying tended to be a barrier to transfer. Recovering memories from deceased brains was like recovering data from a hard drive that had been through the microwave. They don't permit that kind of software in the box. If a transfer took place within minutes of death, it could theoretically succeed, but the window was small and conflicted with timelines reserved for resuscitation. Besides, I wanted in the box because I didn't want to die. The whole idea of a D-15 contradicted that.

I delved deeper into the list, looking for flights of slightly more realistic fancy. Eleven-point-six mil for killing some guy's ex-wife. Ten-nine for the experience of being mauled by three Dobermans and a Chihuahua. The most lucrative were always the least sane.

I scrolled down a bit further. Eight-six for walking a high wire over the Strait of Gibraltar. Seven-seven for winning a bar fight against three or more rednecks wielding pool cues — an idea intriguing in its specificity. Alas, my talents were not pugilistic in nature.

Finally I found one that fit my taste. A woman from Bangkok (not that location meant anything) was willing to pay seven-point-one to climb the American Statue of Liberty from toe to crown using magnets on her hands and knees — rather, on my hands and knees. Nevermind that the copper statue was not magnetic. Far be it from me to deny the lady her wish.

I immediately began researching the feasibility of the stunt, beginning with the structure of the statue. As suspected, Lady Liberty's internal framework was in fact iron. Better magnetism. The statue could be climbed as long as I followed her rivets. All I needed now was sufficient gear.

I was an experienced climber, but I had no idea how to acquire powerful electromagnets. I had an idea who might know. I frowned. I really didn't want to call Chelsea.

miranda7: looks like Ive finally got some1 to fulfill my desire
LucAs: which is that??
miranda7: the big 1
miranda7: the 1 you said Id never b able 2 get
LucAs: r u serious?? i still cant blieve its possible!!
LucAs: what psycho is gonna do that??
miranda7: not gonna
miranda7: already did
miranda7: some thrill hoarder named Chang
miranda7: hes supposed 2 b transferring as we speak
miranda7: cant wait 2 xperience it
LucAs: waiting…
LucAs: always seems like 10 fleshtimes when ur waiting for a memory!!
miranda7: and you arent helping a damn bit

"Look who crawled out from under his rock and finally called me," Chelsea said into the cam, her face twisted as if she had eaten some bad protein. Then she hung up.

Not bad. I had anticipated an even cooler reception. I reestablished the link, this time with a small bouquet of dying flowers in hand. The old lady next door had thrown them onto the incinerator pile, but they looked pleasant enough from a distance.

Chelsea was in mid-sentence when her image shot back to life. "—ass hole, you blew your shot when—" She paused to study my pathetic little smile and handful of flora. "Aw, damn you Chang." She examined every inch of me on her screen. "Flowers aren't even trembling. That's good. So the M.S.—"

"I keep things in check."

Her weight shifted, then back. "Fine, what do you want?"

I leaned forward and kissed the cam. "Chelsea, babe, you're the queen."

Her eyebrows arched. "This doesn't mean I'm sleeping with you again."

Something in her voice suggested she might not be as serious in that conviction as she wanted me to believe. I filed the thought away, but my current matter took precedence.

"I need to get my hands on some electromagnets," I told her.

"Technically, I need to get my hands and knees on them."

Chelsea settled into a chair constructed of old wooden crates. She was about as affluent as I was, with aspirations in line with my own. We were part of the same societal underbelly. "Let me guess," she said, "Liberty Island?"

My smile disintegrated. "How did you know?"

"Axel made the same request about two weeks back. Want me to tell you the same I told him?"

"Preferably something better."

"Well, I told him magnets designed for handling sheet metal should work fine. There's a few places on the commercial net to order electromags like that."

"How much do they run?"

"Quite a bit."

"Hmm. I was looking for something closer to free."

Chelsea laughed a single syllable. "You really haven't changed a bit." She placed a finger on her temple and sat silently for a good minute. I let her think. She was more active in the shady circles than I was. If she was trying to devise a method for me to acquire magnets in my price range, my input could only slow her down.

A mischievous smile crept to her lips as an idea took shape. "What if I could arrange for Axel's shipment to be redirected to you?"

"I doubt Axel would appreciate that."

"He wouldn't." Chelsea shrugged. "You didn't appreciate it when he borrowed your chute in Paris, did you?"

"That was Axel?" Bastard cost me a spot in the largest simultaneous Eiffel base jump in history. Of course, three jumpers died when their lines tangled and French police arrested eighteen of the thirty-seven daredevils, so perhaps I owed him thanks. Or maybe just payback. "Do it."

LucAs: how u holding up??
miranda7: Im getting impatient
miranda7: I paid a lot of $ to get Chang in here 4 that memory
miranda7: and now hes in a secure network
miranda7: they wont even give ME access
LucAs: those memories might b unsafe!!
miranda7: y would they b unsafe
LucAs: y u think??

miranda7:…
LucAs: ???
miranda7: Ill get it anyway

I didn't know how Chelsea did it — I didn't want to know — but a set of four twenty-five pound electromagnets addressed to Alex Goldstein showed up at my door by three that afternoon. Twenty-five pounds each? How was I going to haul an extra hundred pounds up that monument?

I left the apartment with the magnets but without a satisfactory solution. By the time I reached the airport I had concluded that the weight of the magnets would be negligible since they would be adhered to the statue most of the time, making their weight less my problem and more Lady Liberty's. I just hoped I could convince my muscles as easily as I convinced my brain.

I managed to snag a free flight to New York as a jumpseat-paramedic. I kept my EMT license current for such occasions when a jumpseat might be useful. Allowing paramedics free flights saved airlines the millions it would cost to train their flight crew for medical emergencies and fifty times that in lawsuit payouts. Only once had a passenger required my services during a flight. I managed to stabilize the elderly heart attack victim until we reached the ground. Heroic memories played well in the box, but not like the crazy ones did.

This flight was uneventful, as was the bus ride from the airport. The ferry, on the other hand…

I boarded the 11:30 ferry to Liberty Island just as the gate was closing. That is to say I jumped over a rail onto the boat while the ticket taker's attention was on the gate. A few people noticed, but it didn't matter. New York tourists had neither the time nor inclination to tattle on a freeloader.

The jump was quite a feat considering the hundred pounds of magnets on my back. The bag shifted as I landed, and a heavy corner bounced against me. The impact was barely an inch from my spine. The pain danced outward in concentric rings only to leap back to the center and begin again.

I collapsed into the nearest bench, my chest heaving. There was nothing I could do for the back, but I gave myself a subcutaneous to stave off spasms the M.S. liked to produce at inopportune times. Then I took my first good look at my objective.

I had never seen Lady Liberty in person before. The high morning sun cast practically no shadow from her flowing green gown. Her majesty overshadowed the natural beauty of the harbor and even the magnificence of the metropolis behind her. It was the one and only time I bothered to savor her beauty. Once I reached the island, she would be little more than a new dare.

I only stopped ogling her when a different visage caught my eye, one more personally familiar and far less pleasing to behold. The greasy black hair. The J-shaped scar that swept across the broad nose and turned up at his left eye. The pointed stud protruding from his lower lip like a drool pimple. The face recognized me back. His ugly mouth formed my name as I silently spoke his: "Axel."

Axel's pack seemed as bulky as mine. Where had he gotten magnets? Or were my magnets never intended for Axel? Chelsea probably purchased them with a hot credit account. She knew I didn't roll that way. Like I said, she was shadier than I was. Sneakier, too.

I tried to play it casual. Too direct a charge off the boat would be suspicious, perhaps grounds for arrest. As it stood I preferred not having my bag searched. Unfortunately, Axel was not renowned for his subtlety. I needed to make it to the monument before he inspired an island-wide lockdown. My heart quickened. My muscles tensed.

Axel and I ended up shoulder to shoulder beside the gate when the ferry pulled up to the dock. Axel's patience broke early. He thrust his elbow into my sternum, threw a foot onto the rail, and launched himself the final four yards to the pier. He landed running.

I suppressed an urge to follow. I had seen too many second jumpers get taken down. Besides, Axel had knocked the wind out of me. I simply had to wait this scene out. Good thing I did.

Axel toppled to the ground under the influence of the fastest moving rent-a-cop I had ever seen. Two others arrived quickly, one helping to restrain, the other removing Axel's duffle. Two city officers helped divert tourists from the scene. It was one of the few times I found myself impressed with a security force.

I hung back on the ferry while the first few passengers scurried onto the island. They were too preoccupied with the scene to notice anything else. I smirked as I strolled past the struggle. Axel would surely put up a good fight. I had plenty of time.

miranda7: I told you Id get it
LucAs: u got it??
LucAs: how??

miranda7: shared a few files with some1
LucAs: who??
miranda7: what do u care
LucAs: i dont
LucAs: who??
miranda7: i got some hacking memories from him
LucAs: a him??
miranda7: jealous
LucAs: not quite
LucAs: so u hacked the secure system??
miranda7: yes
LucAs: dont u know thats illegal??
miranda7: yes
miranda7: I just wish I still had adrenaline
miranda7: that always made breaking the law more fun

I ducked a security screening and blended with the tourists as far as the top tier of the pedestal. That still left a very tricky twenty vertical feet between me and Libby's massive green toes. There were few climbing opportunities: the rail was too far from the statue to be useful, the walls were sheer, and magnets didn't seem likely to adhere to stone. I hurled the backpack up and looked for a way to follow.

I ended up commandeering a doorway which I climbed with an extended chimney technique until I could reach the top of a carved eave. It didn't offer much of a handhold, but it worked to pull myself up. I had one minor slip but found myself standing on oxidized copper in short order.

I looked down. A significant crowd was already gathering and not a single magnet had touched Libby's heel, a surprising number of them dressed in white, almost as if a team of medics had been standing by, waiting for someone to do something this stupid. A familiar tingle of profundity danced through my spine. I loved an audience. But Axel's captors were also watching, brainstorming methods to get me into the patrol car beside him.

"No rest for the weary," I told a nearby pigeon. She fluttered away without response.

I strapped on my gear as quickly as I could. My arms were already feeling like half-cooked spaghetti. My fingers ached from the tiny ledges. My back still throbbed. I ignored the pain, found a rivet, and started climbing before lactic acid set in.

The first clunk of magnet-on-toga was loud, hollow, and very satisfying. Rhythm found me quickly. Press the knee button, flip the thumb switch, raise the leg, reach with the arm, flip the hand magnet on, jam the knee magnet on. Then repeat with the other hand and leg. The magnet's tiny vibrations in my hands almost tickled, offset by the thump that accompanied each reach. Knee-switch-leg-reach-switch-knee. Knee-switch-leg-reach-switch-knee. The pattern was actually quite dull.

Dull or not, it was hard work. The sweat on my palms made the rocker switches more and more difficult to operate. It also made the magnets harder to hold. I was almost to the statue's tucked left elbow before my rhythm finally broke.

The mistake came in the middle of a sequence. I pushed the knee button, flicked the rocker switch, raised the leg...hit the thumb switch again, then tried to reach up. The result: my left hand-magnet stuck in the folds of that enormous toga before I was ready. My hand slipped away and I was stretching an empty palm above my head. Oops. At least the magnet was still stuck to the surface. I reached for it. Another oops. I hit the rocker switch before my grip was secure. The device was at my navel by the time I realized I had lost it. I watched it fall, bounce off the statue's base, shatter to bits on the pavement below.

I hung there a few moments in awe of my clumsiness. The air was cooler up here than it had been on the ground. For a moment I heard my pigeon friend flutter past. Then nothing. Nothing but the mild wind around me. It was peaceful, free, like the air before a base jump. Only here I wasn't free; I was as trapped on this statue as in a cage.

Now what?

My muscles grew tighter and more exhausted every second I pondered my predicament. Could I climb any further with only one hand magnet? Could I climb down that way? I grabbed the remaining hand-mag in both fists and adjusted my grip. It hadn't been designed with two hands in mind.

Up seemed somehow easier than down. I flicked the rocker and summoned all my ab strength in a vertical lunge, reengaging the magnet as my stretch reached its peak. It worked. One at a time I hauled my legs up into something resembling the fetal position. I lunged again.

It was slower than my original rhythm and a lot more awkward, but the inchworm technique had me making progress again. I was above the top of

Liberty's tablet when a tremor overtook me.

It was in my left forearm. Like a distant cousin of the sneeze, a trembling urge for a sudden and violent jolt. I fought it as long as I could, but the arm-sneeze would not be denied. At last I gave in to it, focusing on my other hand, my grip, as the small seizure erupted through my arm, slinging like I was trying to shake off a spider web.

It passed. I placed my hand back on the magnet. My whole body sighed in relief.

Oh no.

The entire weight of my body was suddenly jerking at my shoulder sockets. Both knees drifted away from the statue. Idiot. All my focus had been on my hands, ignoring my knees enough to let them relax and trigger their switches, disengaging both magnets. Or had it been the MS, a separate tremor? Impossible to tell. It mattered little now.

Green metal scrolled slowly upward as the only engaged magnet slid under my weight. I listened to the grating of metal on metal above my head. The friction vibrated my palms, making my fingers itch. Between the sweat, the itching, the pain…

The magnet slipped from my grasp. The air around me accelerated. The lovely green metal drifted away. I had always loved freefall. I tried to enjoy it. The sound of air flying past. The sense of weightlessness. The breeze. The anticipation.

There was a flash when the back of my head found the pain. My body recoiled and the world tumbled over. My face struck the stone base. I didn't feel anything after that. I couldn't see. I heard the blood rush to my head — and out of it. I could taste the heat from the fluids pouring out my mouth. I smelled the sea.

Then it all just faded away.

Perfect blackness in all five senses.

It was beautiful.

LucAs: so u really got your D-15
LucAs: how was it??
miranda7: it was beautiful
miranda7: it was so
miranda7: real
LucAs: little 2 real 4 that chang kid!!

miranda7: chang was compensated

LucAs: for all the good it did him

miranda7: so his program is still in quarantine

LucAs: indefinitely

miranda7:

LucAs: was it worth it??

miranda7: you mean the 15 mil

miranda7: or the 2 mil for the standby transfer team @ liberty island

LucAs: all of it. was it worth the price??

miranda7: it was a D-15

miranda7: worth every penny

Thinking Out Loud

Parks

I felt no pain when I woke that morning. It was the first entirely pain free morning since I left G-block, more likely since before my incarceration. Like most mornings, I sat up on the cot, scratched my head, and rediscovered the ceramic jelly jar protruding from my skull. Still there. Absence of pain did not imply absence of implant.

I staggered across my roomy twelve-by-nine cell to the mirror over the toilet-sink. The reflection offered no surprises. My tan was a shade lighter, the stubble on my scalp a modicum thicker, the humanity in my eye a candela dimmer. What else was I losing in this hellhole? Intellect, wit, social prowess? Whoever decided prison was not cruel and inhuman lacked the humanity necessary to make the determination.

I cocked my head to better survey the reflection of Dr. Waverly's handiwork. It hadn't changed since yesterday. The oblong cylinder bulged from the back-left quadrant of my head, rounding out just short of my neck. I'd had hangovers that felt like I looked. A pink halo of new flesh surrounded the ceramic mass. And I'd volunteered for this? But what other contribution to science was I making from gen-pop of the Alabama State Penitentiary?

When I couldn't look at that pale weakling any longer, I snatched up the remote from the table. I held it in front of me for a few seconds but just tossed it back on the bed. For all the perks built into the research wing's "luxury cells" — single occupancy, television, meals that actually resembled food, mattress with a passing resemblance to comfort, a toilet no other prisoner could see — it was still a cell. HBO wasn't going to make that go away. Still, anything was better than spending a half hour squirting diarrhea for an audience of a half dozen skinheads and a guy named Tickler. Privacy was priceless.

Privacy. I should have asked more questions.

A reverberating clank announced the opening of the magnetic hatch at the end of the cellblock. The door eased back on its massive hinges to reveal C.O. Balantine escorting another man whose crisp green uniform mocked Balantine's rumpled gray. A military man. About time. We were their pet project, after all. By the collection of ribbons and pins on his chest, I judged his rank high. His crisp footfalls echoed down the corridor as they approached.

"Hell if I know how they're doing," Ballantine said in response to a question I hadn't heard. "Fine, I guess. The squirrelly guy had stomachaches since he transferred in." He meant Shipiro. None of the others in this block could be thought squirrelly. "We keep him stocked with Alka-Seltzer and he don't complain so much."

The military man clicked his tongue in irritation. "He had a five-inch needle of adrenaline jabbed in his heart two weeks ago, the only thing that kept him from dying on the operating table. A little bellyache is the least of his problems. Keep an extra close eye on that one."

I almost died? No one told me.

The squirrel was awake.

I always saw myself more a ferret.

"Good," the green officer said in a louder voice, a voice directed toward me. His eyes tracked automatically to the gray mass. "We seem to have at least one early riser."

I stumbled to my feet while he sized me up. The tension in the corners of his mouth suggested he was less than thrilled with what he saw.

"Am I supposed to salute or something?" I asked at last. I just wanted the guy to stop staring at my gut.

The green man forced a laugh. "Nothing like that is necessary, Mr. Parks."

"Doctor."

"Excuse me?"

"It's Doctor Parks. You said mister."

A smile every bit as false as the laugh crept to the man's lips. "Of course it is. How you feeling, Doctor? Any dizziness, anything like that?"

"I had a vivid dream about a fat Dominican girl, does that count?"

She Puerto Rican, joto. Muerte was awake, too.

"No, it doesn't."

"Then I'm fine."

Balantine presented a set of cuffs and leg irons. Field trip. Goody. I stepped to the bars and let the guard reach through and fasten them. They weren't as snug as usual.

Again I felt the green man's eyes boring into that thing they had put in my skull. I couldn't have felt more exposed if he were staring at my genitals. I tried to divert his focus.

"I didn't catch your name, Lieutenant." I hoped the sarcasm in my voice covered the nervousness.

"Lieutenant?" he scoffed. "Try General. Crouch. I'll be supervising the experiments."

Ooh, a general! I better wear my dress socks. Is he staying for supper? I bet they'll let him use metal utensils.

"So we start today?" I asked.

"Assuming you're up to it."

"I'll have to clear my calendar; that will only take a few minutes. Just let me call my secretary."

"Don't get cheeky, Parks," Balantine said. He was trying to sound threatening. Having heard real threats from the guard, I was unimpressed by the affectation.

Crouch raised a palm to Balantine like he was calling off a dog. "No harm done. I could use a good laugh every now and then." He didn't laugh. "This won't take more than a few hours. I'll have the good professor back for his afternoon appointments."

Balantine swiped his card through the panel outside my door, his face clenched like he was experiencing an ice cream headache. My cell swung open. He clasped my shoulder, fingers digging into pressure points warningly, and conducted me out. We moved — slowly considering the baby steps the irons restricted me to — deeper into the research wing, toward the other three guinea pigs. Two of them were awake, only Fowler yet to make his presence known. I hadn't met any of the others in person, but I knew them. Knew their faces, their voices, their daydreams, their nightmares. And they knew me, in ways no one on the outside ever knew me, ways no people were ever meant to know one another.

We passed a few empty cells before reaching the first inmate.

"Armando Muerte," Balantine announced when the man came into view. "Born in Cuba, ended up in Miami, big surprise. Ran there with the Latin Kings long enough to build a record, then moved to Birmingham to set up a franchise. Built up two strikes before—"

"I am well aware of Mr. Muerte's transgressions, Officer," Crouch said. "If he played well with others, he wouldn't be here at all, would he?"

Of course Crouch would have read full dossiers on all four of us. He would know all of Muerte's offenses as well as the man's height, weight, eye color, psych profile, maybe even his real last name. Excluding the last, I knew these things about Muerte, too. I knew that Muerte's current sentence was for gunning down two rival gang members from his Escalade. A seven year old girl happened to be in the apartment behind the targets and also took a fatal bullet. *That was accidente.* Three consecutive life terms.

But everything I knew of Muerte still didn't prepare me for the actual sight of him. He was without question the largest Latino I had ever seen. *That's right, ese. Grande and mean.* He was easily six-six with biceps like heavily tattooed Christmas hams. He certainly looked like a drive-by murderer.

So it like that? What about you, joto? What you in for? Jaywalking?

It was a completely different experience to hear someone's thoughts as he looked me in the eye. Disquieting. The feeling stayed with me even after I'd shuffled out of Muerte's eye line.

"Which one is this?" Crouch asked as we reached the next cell. The occupant was still in his bed, rolled up in his blanket tight as a Cuban cigar. *What that supposed to mean, ese?*

Balantine tapped the bars with his baton. The cigar cringed. "T.J. Fowler," Balantine told Crouch, "our resident jewel thief. Softest of the bunch. He was a popular little guy in gen-pop. Volunteered hisself just so he could sit comfortable again. Want I should wake him?"

"Thank you for your eloquent analysis, but no," Crouch said. "Let him sleep. We'll use him tomorrow."

Not asleep. Pain still so bad. Don't want to go anywhere.

Balantine was dead-on in his assessment of Fowler's motivation. It took no more than an hour to learn Fowler was a hypochondriac and would never elect surgery unless it was to remove some diseased organ from his body, never to put something in. But given the option between thing put into his body, he opted for the military experiment.

There were two cells past Fowler's. A greasy face was pressed to the bars of the furthest. His left index finger swept along the bars like they were chimes, adding a percussive counterbeat to my shuffling footsteps.

Oh, I see him! Damn, Parks is flabbier than I expected. Somewhat warped self-image, Parksey?

If my denial over a few gained pounds suggested a warped self-image, then Shipiro saw himself in a funhouse mirror. He thought himself a late nineteen seventies Jack Nicholson. He looked more like Eddie Haskell on meth, young and twitchy.

Young? He couldn't know I'm only nineteen. Shipiro's teeth clenched. *Dammit!*

"So this must be the infamous Michael Shipiro," Crouch announced as they reached the last cell. *Sweet! I'm infamous now. Think that can get me Knicks tickets on the fifty yard line?* "Alka-Seltzer you said? Any other issues with him?"

Balantine scoffed. "Other than his invisible rabbit named Eli?" *He's a rabbi, not a rabbit. Am I surrounded by morons?* "Been a model cartoon character."

Shipiro stood straight and slapped himself in the forehead in what must have been a mock salute. "Good morning, General. Locked, loaded, and ready for action. Hoo-yaa!"

Crouch studied Shipiro's sweaty face for half a minute. "He'll do," he declared at last. "Get Parks squared away and come back for this one."

Crouch continued to a door at the end of the research wing, Balantine and I a few paces behind. Balantine ran his card again and the door slid to reveal a room smaller than my luxury cell. A single chair sat bolted to the center of the floor, a monitor mounted to the ceiling. Balantine shoved me inside and the door slid again, leaving me alone. As alone as I could be, anyway, with the enormous mirror on one wall. Subtle. I took my seat and stared at the mirror wondering who other than Crouch would be staring back.

Just a chair? Shipriro thought. I was getting good at recognizing who was who in my head. *No guns or tanks or grenades or video games or paintball or Napoleon mini-battlefield or nothing? What kind of military research is this? It's like we're in prison or something.*

Shipiro was shackled and led to a room identical to mine, monitor, mirror and all. I knew this because Shipiro knew this. I was growing accustomed to observing things I didn't actually see. It had been disconcerting at first. The image I received when Muerte first came online was one of his tattoos: a devil extending its middle finger.

A voice came through the monitor's speaker. "Greetings, gentlemen." It was a nasal voice, northern probably, definitely not an Alabama native. "As I suspect you have deduced for yourselves, the devices implanted in your heads are prototype communicators that transmit your thoughts directly from mind to mind. Now we must ascertain the extent of that communication." Male but not masculine, with an arrogance that might have been one of my university colleagues talking to a waiter. It could only be Dr. Waverly.

I was well acquainted with Waverly's reputation, both through research journals and CNN. The interrogation scandal twelve years ago had all fallen in his lap, though he could hardly have been responsible for all of it. Reports suggested he was cooling his heels in some federal country club. It hadn't taken long to realize this was the same Waverly. Not long, but long enough. Had I made the connection before I signed my brain away, I'd probably still be on G-block. He had a reputation for pushing his experiments beyond the boundaries of good science, and neurologists made very scary mad scientists.

"The test is simple," Waverly continued. "Mr. Parks, we will start with you. When—"

"It's Doctor Parks," I snapped. This mister thing was getting out of hand. *Why don't you cry about it?* "I have Ph.D.'s in physics and mathematics. I'm quite certain I've earned the title, in or out of prison." *You tell that científico loco!* "I also think I deserve more consideration for my cooperation than I've received."

More consideration? The words spilled unbidden from my lips. But they were out there, so perhaps…

"Mr. Parks, we are not here to negotiate."

Dude, he's still calling you mister.

What to ask for? "Research journals." It was the first thing to pop in my head. "I'm an important man in my field and I need to continue my research." I pressed my face to the mirror and cupped my hands for shade, but still saw nothing. "And stop putting onions in the meatloaf. I hate that."

"Do you realize that interfering with a military experiment is a federal offense?" It was Crouch's voice.

I forced a chuckle reminiscent of his earlier one. "Throw me in jail, General."

At least you're calling him by the appropriate title.

The voice coming through the speaker changed again. It had been a while since I'd been blessed with Warden Lockheart's gutteral drawl. "Don't want no trouble, Parks, so I makes ya deal. You and 'Piro pull off this here speriment, ya can have yer damn books. A'ight?"

My jaw went slack. Lockheart had never conceded anything to any inmate. A simple request for softer toilet paper had confined my first cellmate to solitary for a week. Compromise from Lockheart was like eggs from a rooster.

And the meatloaf?

"And the meatloaf?"

Shipiro's thought leapt from my lips. Lockheart's temper was legend. Even now the speaker was spewing a string of angry consonants that would have made Dr. Seuss blush. "A'ight," Lockheart finally gasped. "No damn onion. Now straighten up!"

"Mr. Parks," Waverly's voice said again. I was too flustered to correct him. "An image is about to appear on your screen. Focus on it. Mr. Shipiro…"

"That's Doctor Shipiro. I never once lit the nose when playing Operation." I was fairly certain he said it aloud, but Waverly did not react.

"…tell me what Mr. Parks sees."

Like a test for psychics. Cute.

The monitor hummed and an image faded to its surface.

"That would be the letter Y."

It was. Shipiro articulated it before I had the label in my mind. Was he thinking for me? It was the devil tattoo all over again. My stomach churned.

"Four plus three."

The number seven had appeared on the screen. Of course Shipiro responded with his signature zaniness. It was exhausting to have that in my head all the time.

The images kept coming, as did Shipiro's correct answers. They became more complex as we continued. Upside-down smiley face. Seventeen stars around a crescent moon. The Canadian flag. Richard Nixon. The decimal for the square root of two over two.

Really? How the hell did a guy who thought Kermit was a real frog recognize point-seven-zero-seven-one as half the square root of two? I hadn't thought beyond the decimal. How deep was he digging? Get this fruit loop out of my head!

The image changed. I tried to think of something else. *"Cat on a doghouse."* Too late.

It changed again. I looked away and focused on the first image to drift into my mind: Muerte's tattoo. "Satan giving the finger," I muttered to myself. "Satan giving the finger."

"No," Shipiro said. Of course I didn't hear him, but I might as well have. *"Parks, you have your Christian mythology all wrong. It's not Satan. That's Charlie Brown."*

How could he know? I never looked at the screen. I still wasn't looking at it; I was facing the one-way window. But there it was. It never strayed into my conscious mind until Shipiro's proclamation: the round head and black on yellow zig-zag of Charlie Brown reflected in the mirror.

I was experiencing the dizziness Crouch had asked about earlier. Fortunately, this was the last of the images. I was escorted back to my cell just in time to vomit into my private toilet. *When did you eat corn?* Yeah, private.

As an added bonus, Warden Lockheart personally delivered my dinner. Meatloaf. "Eat up, smart ass," Lockheart commanded. He wasn't leaving until I did. I took a bite.

The texture was stiff, grainy. I used the plastic fork to fillet the loaf. There were shreds of paper in it. I didn't have to read the word "theorem" off the largest shred to realize Lockheart had made good on both promises: the meatloaf's onions had been replaced by pages from my research journal. He watched until I had eaten every bite.

Fowler

I understood Parks' discomfort with the whole situation. There were things in my head that no one needed to know. Simply knowing that people might see them made it that much harder to not think about them, and thinking about them sure made it more likely that someone was going to see them.

No one wants to be in your brain when your thoughts chase their own asses like that.

Good, you can just stay out.

The general came for me the second day, which meant I was expected to let people in enough to complete the experiment. I didn't want to be difficult, but I didn't like people being in my head. The very idea is just so…what's the word?

Wierd?

Uncomfortable?

Loco?

Stop it!

The room was exactly as I'd envisioned it, probably because it was exactly how Parks saw it, though a small table bearing a large round button had been added. I felt an immediate urge to push the button, but I hadn't been told to, so I didn't. Oh, I wanted to. I'd never wanted to push a button so much in my life. I'm not sure it was my own impulse that drove me, but it was my will that resisted.

Muerte arrived in the second room and the button urge tripled. He had a button and was already pushing the daylights out of it. Surely we'd be pushing the buttons eventually. There was no need to be hasty. The urge lessened with the thought, but it did not disappear.

"Today's experiment deals with timing," said the doctor's voice through the television. "Our first exercise will be synchronization. One of you will hear a beep. When he does, you will both push your buttons. We will be measuring the time that elapses between your respective actions as well as the time elapsed between the beep and each response. Are your directions clear?"

"Push the button when it beeps?" I said. "Think I can handle that, boss."

Suck up.

It was a boring task. Nothing but beep-press, beep-press. The first few times I was aware of Muerte's efforts to time his button with mine, but soon he blended into a shadow of my own thoughts. It was as if my mind was guiding his hand as well as my own. Maybe it was.

Or worse, maybe his guided mine.

Two hours passed with variation after variation: pushing with left and right hands, pushing with our feet, our noses, him with one body part and me with another, even running across the room to the button. It was quite a relief when I heard the hiss of the sliding door instead of another beep. I hoped my contribution to the experiment was beneficial. I also desired to never see another button as long as I lived.

I returned to my cell to find Parks thinking about me. It was the first time I'd been the subject of someone else's thought. And Parks had felt exposed when Crouch stared at his implant?

So jewels, Parks thought at me almost conversationally. *How does one get into that?*

Other than Muerte, none of us thought much on our crimes. I knew Shipiro was some sort of mad bomber. How did he get into that? How did Muerte end up a gang banger? How did Parks get into…professoring?

Math and science are what I was good at. I studied to get better, got my PhDs. Becoming a professor was the next step.

Not so different from me then.

You like jewels that much?

Jewels? Did people play hockey because they liked the Stanley Cup? No, because they loved the game. And I loved the game, the challenge of defeating the most intricate security systems the western world had to offer.

Hate to tell you, you're in the most elaborate security system in the west. Forget breaking in, break out.

Break out? That was the stupidest thing I'd ever heard. We were under such tight watch that we couldn't even discuss the idea, let alone do it.

What we doing now, ese?

Muerte

El día next, they took me to the room with el mirror. They hung una blackboard inside, with chalk to write. ¿Why they do this? *Math.* I not know.

Muerte, pay attention. They want you to do math.

¿Matemática? No good at matemática. Armando flunked grade six. Tres times.

Relax, I passed the third grade. Lockheart and Balantine are coming for me.

Parks thought like Armando not know. Parks spent all his time thinking of warden's meatloaf stunt. But Parks would play along with la charade. It was importante they think nothing suspicious happening. We follow direcciónes to our best. They gave Parks un book and told him to have Armando work una problema.

"*¿Is that it?*" Parks said to el doctor loco. "*¿A homogeneous linear equation with constant coefficients? I assume you want the general solution.*" Then at me he think, *¿Why are you just standing there like a moron?*

I know you not thinking that at me, joto.

Pick up the chalk. Go to the board and write this.

I picked up la chalk but no comprende what he wanted Armando to write. It not sound even like matemática. ¿Letters?

I'm looking at it. ¿Shipiro knew Charlie Brown from a reflection but you can't copy this?

Charlie Brown makes sense. This es loco.

Just do it.

I could not. I try, but made no sense. My músculos tensed. I wanted to break everything. La chair. La blackboard. El mirror. Everything I could find.

Maybe the big guy is thinking too hard. Could cause brain damage.

Now I wanted to break Shipiro.

¿Could Shipiro be right?

It would be a first.

Try it.

I lost track of who think what en mi cabeza.

Muerte, this was Parks, *just relax. Let your hand work, but don't think about it. Like when you do chest reps, just let your body do the work by itself.*

Chest reps. That Armando comprende. I did fifty en la morning and fifty en la noche. I do so many I not have to try hard. I missed the weights en el yard.

My hand started writing en la blackboard. ¿What was I doing?

Just let it go. Don't think about it.

I no think. My hand kept working. El hand worked for cinco minutes before it draw circle around la answer.

They gave Parks another problema. He stared at it for un moment. *That'll take forever to work by hand. I need a calculator.*

¡Perfect! ¿Can you get one with an infrared port?

I'll ask. Parks banged on his mirror and demanded un calculator. "*It needs to be a graphing calculator. And get a Hewlett-Packard. I don't want one of those TI's. I'd have an easier time solving the damn thing with a GameBoy.*"

It was una hour before el calculator arrived. Me and Parks worked mas problemas while we waited. The others used el time to discuss why we needed el calculator. Armando no comprende most of it. They tell me it no matter.

While they talked, I remembered Parks never tell Armando why he en prisión.

None of your damn business.

But he thought about it. He came to prison over una chica. But he no love her. He think about her pechos. Her piernas. Her culo. He had thoughts about this niña like Armando has about chicas de Puerto Rico. But Parks no just think, he remembered.

He remembered that the girl did not like it.

I'm gonna be sick.

Don't be a pussy, Fowler.

¿Did you see how young she was? Seventeen. She was seventeen when Parks raped her.

¿You're judging me? All of you are judging me. ¿You three in here for skipping jury duty?

¿Was she la only one?

Girls did me favors to raise their grades. Never bothered any of them before. Una lie. Parks was thinking of tres niñas with tears en their eyes. Latino men no make chicas cry. You tell yourself that. Parks may be worst of us all.

So much worse than gunning down a child.

"Inmate Muerte," a real voice said, "palms on the glass." It took un minute to recognize who was talking to Armando. Warden Lockheart. I walked to la window and leaned in position. La door slid open, un guard came in, calculator dropped en la chair, and guard left.

That was sloppy guard work, Fowler thought. *Missed opportunity.*

Not yet, Shipiro thought. *The timing isn't right. Got to play this smart.* For once, Shipiro no sound loco.

I was already prodding el calculator and scratching la chalk across la blackboard. Nothing made sense, so I ignore again. I listened to the others' thoughts.

They'll want the calculator back. This isn't going to work.

It will work if they don't want it.

¿You mean a distraction?

I mean break the calculator. They won't want a busted calculator.

¿What are we going to do with a broken calculator?

Leave that to me.

¿And me? ¿What part did Armando play?

¿Isn't it obvious? You have to break the calculator. I grabbed el calculator en both hands. ¡*Not until the math is finished! We have to keep cooperating.* I relaxed grip, let Parks control my hand again.

It no take long to finish la matematica. Then el voice del doctor came again. "Congratulations, Mr. Muerte, you've just done calculus."

Break it now.

I leapt up and yelled like I won la Copa Mundial. "¡And you pendejos thinked I was estupido!" I spiked el calculator into la floor. I raised my arms and danced la rumba frenetica.

El door slid open. Four guards rushed in. *¡The calculator! ¡Get the calculator!* Un guard jumped on my back. He was light. I stood over el calculator before another grabbed me. I fell on el calculator and stuffed los pieces en my pantalones. I missed some pieces, but Shipiro said they no importante. I let los guards cuff me and drag me back to my cell, laughing like un hyena and struggling enough that they no want to search me.

I no comprende el plan, but I was part of it.

Shipiro

Muerte made an easy puppet. Even in the dark and working under his blankets, both of which slowed my work considerably, it only took a few hours to dismantle the calculator and television remote to make my exit device. Technically Muerte made it, but that was only semantics. He never could have done anything without me. None of them could.

A drive-by gang thug, a cat burgling jewelry lover, and a rapist with a Ph.D. Quite the motley crew I'd fallen in with. Parks thought himself the brains of this outfit. Ha! Let him enjoy that delusion. As if he'd had a single thought I hadn't had first. If anything, he proved the most useless of them all. Fowler's expertise with security systems was the catalyst to the whole endeavor. Muerte's muscle was going to prove essential before the end. Parks contributed much more to the generals' work than to ours. If nothing else, he could be the fall guy if this didn't work.

I wasn't worried about the others overhearing my thoughts the way I eavesdropped on theirs. They hadn't yet penetrated my secret to privacy:

insanity. That was all they heard, the random murmurs that drifted around my cranial cavity. I just pushed them to the fore, even whispering them aloud. "I like butter on my Corn Flakes." Or "If they make boots out of shark skin, why not jellyfish?" Or song lyrics. An interesting sounding word over and over, like "marsupial" or "blatherskite". The map from the third level of Mario Brothers. The time I saw my grandmother naked. Anything they didn't want to share was what I offered, leaving my real thoughts in the subconscious. Even now I was listing the names of all the Care Bears I could remember. Good Luck Bear was always my favorite.

Morning would be the time to act. Guards reacted slower in the morning. They were used to inmates being sluggish getting out of their hard beds in the less-than-silent cellblock. Neither of those things affected us here. Not to mention that we'd be working together far more cohesively than they would. All we needed was a distraction. The needle Parks overheard Crouch mention, the one they jammed into my heart, gave me the idea. That and my stomachaches.

It was still too early to act— the night shift was always more jumpy — when someone else's mind came online. Parks.

Hey, Crazy Bear, you never shared your crime. Don't you ever think about it?

No, I hadn't shared anything I didn't want to. And yes, I thought about it constantly. But it was dangerous to respond to a direct question by thinking about it. I raised my surest defense, a recitation of the movie *The Princess Bride*, out loud.

Anything with wires was my poison. I started with computers, but who gets to see the results of a virus? It lacked the thrill of catastrophe. So I moved to sabotage, first just for fun and eventually for hire. I put a lot of technical companies out of business using their air conditioning systems to start electrical fires. Then it dawned on me that fires were simply slow explosions. Unfortunately, a piece of the rental van I used to plant the bomb in the parking garage of Riverchase Galleria survived the blast enough to trace back to me. Hence my incarceration.

But damn that blast was beautiful.

This boy is an elephant snack.

"As you wish," I muttered.

Shift change, Parks thought. *Everyone on the clock.*

Muerte knew his role. Parks only had to be lookout, at the end of the block like he was. Fowler's job was practically over. My turn. I ripped open two Alka-Seltzers and prepared my performance.

Crouch

A full week into the tests and every one came back better than anticipated. Image and thought transmission were both proven successful. The synchronicity results rivaled factory machinery. That Hispanic Neanderthal worked the math problems like he'd been doing it for years, and with better handwriting. But Waverly promised the C-48 Cerebral Communicator would turn these cons into soldiers. I didn't see it. The C-48 was good, but was it worth the expense? The invasiveness? I was going to have to pull the plug. Enough taxpayer money had been dumped down this hole already.

I entered the prison control room with every intention of telling Waverly it was over. The alarm blaring in the room wiped the thought from my head.

Lockheart was screaming something about a medical emergency into a telephone. His head guard Balantine rushed toward the research block, two medics behind him.

A closer look at the monitor revealed the reason for the chaos. Shipiro was on the floor of his cell twitching like a jackhammer.

My mind flashed to his surgery. The screaming machines. The frantic doctors. The giant needle in his chest. I felt my career slip through my fingers.

Four guards and two medics appeared on the monitor a minute later. "He's foaming at the mouth!" one of the guards shouted over his radio. It took both medics and three guards to roll Shipiro to his side. I didn't realize they'd left Shipiro's cell door open until I saw Muerte walk through it.

The giant Latino's presence surprised the guards, too. He punched one in the face, knocking him cold. He kicked a second in the knee; the man collapsed, his leg doubled under the wrong way.

Lockheart stammered in all consonants as he took off toward the fray. The jailbreak siren roared across the grounds. I could only watch as Muerte throttled the last guard. Shipiro was on his feet now, slapping the hell out of one of the medics.

Muerte tossed something to Shipiro, who dropped the medic and exited the cell. He reappeared on Fowler's camera and fed some sort of circuit board into the door. Fowler's cell swung open. Parks' cell was open a few seconds later.

"Now that is a successful experiment," Dr. Waverly announced triumphantly as the fourth inmate slipped out. My stunned glare turned to Waverly. His grin was bigger than ever. "Come now, General, what did you expect to happen? Fowler's a jewel thief – a security system expert. Muerte's the muscle. Parks, the brains. And I'm certain Shipiro was never what he seemed. You take a group like that, let them talk in a way we can't hear, enable them to share skills…"

"You knew this would happen!"

"Knew?" Waverly asked himself. "Let's say I hoped. All it took was a broken calculator and an Alka-Seltzer. Not bad. And now they've gotten their mitts on Balantine's access card." He blew a low whistle. "What could a team of your Green Berets could do with this stuff? Or SEALS? Force Recon? Of course, those are probably Boy Scouts compared to the teams you'd really give this to."

"What about the guards? What about Lockheart?"

"What about them? It's a shame that those six lost focus in Shipiro's cell, but typically they can handle themselves. Lockheart may talk like Yosemite Sam, but he can control his prison. He'll have this place locked down in an hour. Or not. We have GPS in those implants. They can't get far. And if they do make it past the ravor wire, there's Lockheart's failsafe."

"What failsafe? I don't recall approving a failsafe."

"I didn't ask. It was a deal-breaker for Lockheart. I couldn't risk you saying no."

"What have you done?"

"Relax. It's just a little zap. A fraction of what a tazer delivers. The very definition of non-lethal force."

"A tazer to the brain is non-lethal?"

Waverly shrugged. "Either way, I bet I could get the results published. Under a pseudonym, anyway."

Waverly kept talking through the blaring sirens while I tried to envision my report. Three guards were down, at least one dead. Our four test subjects had used the device to derail the experiment and acquire the means to escape a secure prison facility. Short of Waverly's unauthorized modification, we had not been equipped to deal with such a system. The implants enabled four simple inmates to outclass the US Miltary and the Alabama Department of Corrections.

Clearly the experiment was a complete success.

Zombies

It's all fun and games until someone dies, comes back, and eats your spleen.

Not Rats

Horst and Gunter huddled beside the lone window on the third floor of the tallest and most solidly-built house in Holzminden. The house belonged to neither of them. The owner was in the hallway, fighting to get through the door and kill them. He was also dead. He was joined by more towns-corpses, scratching and pounding and moaning in their mindless struggle to get inside and devour the two living men.

But Horst and Gunter were not looking at the door; they were looking out the window. "There," Horst said suddenly. He pointed at a colorful blotch on the road outside of town. The blotch was not moving away from Holzminden like any intelligent traveler would be, it was approaching. "We need to get out there and meet him."

Gunter released a gurgle of disbelief that could have come as easily from the other side of the door. "Out there? You're off your head."

"We can't just let him wander into town. He'll be torn limb from limb."

"He's got four limbs; we have eight. Do the math." It was likely the first time Gunter had ever tried to use math to his advantage.

"The Piper is the last hope Holzminden has."

A snort. "You believe Holzminden still has hope?" The door banged, accompanied by a series of low moans. Gunter waved an arm toward the sound. "Holzminden is out there. Bloodthirsty and slavering. And dead, by the way. I don't want to be dead. You're not opening that door."

"Door?" Horst looked out the window. The piper was close enough to differentiate his hat from his coat, though both were hideous. "Who said anything about the door?"

Horst ripped apart curtains and linens to fashion a rope. He tied one end to a heavy trunk and dropped the other out the window.

"Off your head," Gunter repeated. He sat on the trunk and crossed his arms, but jumped off again when he heard the wood splinter under his weight. He stood beside the trunk and heard the splintering again. Both men's heads turned, tracking the sound to the door. The splintering repeated and colorless fingers poked into the room.

Gunter was the first out the window, Horst not far behind. Both men hit the ground in a full sprint.

Staying put had clearly been the worst possible idea. Running through town turned out to be a close second. The dead were loitering at every street corner, staggering out of every doorway. It was odd, fleeing their friends and neighbors. They ducked into an alley to avoid Brigitte, the first girl who ever slapped Gunter. Ironically, the hand she had slapped him with was missing. They climbed a fence to escape a noseless Deter von Brut, the first boy to ever punch Horst in the nose. Neither man dared to ponder what was missing from Ingrid, the one woman in town both men had...let's just say it was the most pleasant of the remembered encounters. They actually leapt through a shop's open window and out the back door to avoid her. Both men had gone to similar lengths to avoid Ingrid when she was alive; she had been the possessive type.

Eventually and against all odds, they outran the lumbering corpses and reached the edge of town. Now they had only to find—

"Hello there?" The voice came from just beyond the next hill. "Is someone there?"

"Hello," Horst yelled back.

Gunter slapped a hand over Horst's mouth. "What are you doing? Don't tell it where we are."

Horst pried the fingers away. "Since when do they say hello? Moan? Yes. Gurgle? A bit. But they don't speak."

Gunter skidded to a halt and surveyed his surroundings like a nervous rabbit. "Right. Of course not."

"So this must be..."

The clouds in Gunter's head parted and a ray of realization lit his face. "Piper," he exclaimed as if it was the name of the man cresting the hill. It was the voice he used when talking to old friends he didn't recognize. "So glad you made it. You might just barely be in time to save Holzminden the same way you saved Hamlin."

"Hamlin?" The Piper shook his head. "I'm afraid there's been a misunderstanding. Can we talk—"

Horst and Gunter each grabbed the Piper by an elbow and ushered him off the road and away from the atonal chorus growing in the town behind them. "Talk, yes," Horst said. "But let's walk while we talk."

"Walk quickly," Gunter added. "We can talk quickly, too, if you like, but the walking should definitely be quick."

"A jog even," Horst suggested. "Maybe even a run?"

The piper jerked his arms free and stood his ground. "Is this about the children? Listen, there's been a huge—"

"Misunderstanding," Horst finished for him, seizing the elbow again and resuming the walk. "The bit with the kids isn't a problem. Things get heated during a negotiation. Bygones."

"Bygones," Gunter repeated. "If that magic pipe of yours can lure rats and children, surely it can take care of our little problem. We'll pay anything."

"These aren't rats, mind you." Horst heard a distant moan and gave the Piper's arm and extra little jerk to speed him up. "If a rat bites you, you don't turn into a rat. Nor are they children."

"Some of them are children," Gunter corrected. "Were children, I suppose."

The Piper raised his palms. "Gentlemen, please. The story of Hamlin has been blown out of proportion. For one, I'm not a piper. I have no magic pipe. No pipe at all."

The men blinked.

"Those children that left Hamlin? They followed me out of town because I offered to help them run away. Poor judgment? Perhaps, but they were certainly never entranced. And it wasn't all the children. I think there were seven, ten at the most."

Horst stammered a few incoherent syllables before managing to say, "You're not a piper?"

The colorful man shook his head. "Afraid not."

"What are you then?"

"I play the lute."

"A magic lute?"

"Not even close."

Horst frowned. "You did at least use it to lead the rats out of Hamlin?"

"That's the other bit," the Piper/Lutenist said. "There never were rats in Hamlin."

"But the plague was there. That much I know," said Gunter. "Where there's plague, there's rats."

"Wrong plague." The Piper rubbed his neck. "Turns out Hamlin's plague was brought on by the dead coming back to life and eating the living. Then the people they ate came back to life. The whole thing went on and on. Zombie Plague, I think they called it. Nasty stuff, but not rats."

"So what happened with the zombies?"

"Now that part is true enough. It seems zombies are inexplicably drawn to lute music. So I walked through the streets playing and the zombies followed. I led them to the Weser and they washed downstream."

"So they died?"

The Piper shrugged. "I think they were dead before that. Not really my problem."

This time all three men heard the moaning. It was ahead of them. And behind them. They were surrounded.

"Looks to be your problem now."

"Wait," the Piper said, "are those...zombies? Here? Ah, Holzminden is downstream from— Right. Sorry about that. But are they what you wanted gone?"

"Yes!" Gunter and Horst shouted in chorus.

The Piper brushed his hands on his rainbow clothing. "That I can do."

Horst blew a sigh of relief despite the circle of the quickened corpses of his friends and neighbors tightening around them. "Thank goodness. Go on, then. We'll pay anything, just play."

The Piper removed his hat and scratched his head. "That's the thing, isn't it. Your messenger didn't say anything about bringing my lute. Either of you have one handy?"

ZFL

"It's time again for your weekly dose of mayhem! Chuck Weinstone here with NFL coaching legend and our newest color commentator, Jeff Stevens. We're at the Metrodome where the Detroit Shamblers get set to take on the LA Free-Bleeders. It'll be gruesome. It'll be bloody. It's the ZFL on FOX!

"So Jeff, you're used to a field full of live players. What brings you over to the ZFL?"

"Chuck, football is football, or so my agent says. So here I am."

"And here the Bleeders are, coming off that big win in Houston last week while the Shamblers are looking to snap a three game losing streak. These teams have a long and bitter rivalry; who do you like in this one, Jeff?"

"Chuck, I don't think it's about wins and losses. As long as the fans satisfy their bloodlust, does it really matter?"

"Spoken like a true fan."

"Sure."

"And speaking of fans, who are the lucky superfans in tonight's Donor Seats?"

"It says here that's Steve Clabo and his wife Mar— Dear God! Those are two big, fat—"

"Right you are, Jeff. Two big *fans* donating their blood to make the ball oh-so irresistible to those zombies players."

"Irresistible if the zombies like gravy."

"Zombie football would be nowhere without its fans."

"Wow. Just...wow."

"We all know that zombie players come and go, but it's the living and breathing handlers up in the rafters that really make a game. And we have

117

two of the best tonight in the Shambler's Trey Sogg and LA's 'Zaxter' Zack Baxter. Both are among the elite, but which man-on-the-wire has the advantage tonight?"

"Do we have to do this?"

"It's our job, Jeff."

"Then Sogg."

"You think so?"

"Think about it, Chuck, Zaxter had that field-level harness snag last week in Houston. I don't care how much protective gear the guy's wearing, getting trapped on the field with twenty-two ravenous zombies is going to make him think twice before rappelling in there."

"That was uncomfortable to watch, though you'd never know it from the number of hits that clip got on YouTube. We are assured tonight that the dome's pulley network is one hundred percent operational and our handlers will be zipping through the air like Spider-Man."

"And if not, it's no loss to the gene pool, right Chuck?"

"Now, now, Jeff; this is a family show."

"I sure hope not."

"Both teams are on the field; the handlers are in the air; it's time for dropoff. Just a reminder, this game is brought to you by Machete Zombie Repellent; 'If it's not Machete, you just smell like crap.' Looks like the Bleeders won the toss. The ball's coming out of their chute. Ouch! That dropped right on the shoulder of number twenty-seven, Cliff Murdock."

"Are we really calling the zombies by name? You don't think that makes this even more repugnant?"

"Repugnant? That's a big word, Jeff."

"Especially for our viewers."

"You're doing it again."

"Right, ZFL fans are at the top of the food chain. Or was that the players?"

"There *is* a game going on, Jeff. Number twenty-seven is still trying to pick up the ball, but with his arm dislocated—ooh, make that amputated by the dropping football, he really can't get a grip. That blood makes the ball slippery before it makes it sticky."

"I think I'm gonna be sick."

"Here comes Zaxter swooping in to help. Remember, handlers can touch their own players but not the ball. Interesting strategy; Zaxter is using his player's felled limb to help scoop up the ball."

"What kind of person thinks to do that?"

"A fantastic handler, Jeff, that's who."

"Now your 'fantastic handler' is using that arm to fend off number twenty-seven. Maybe Zaxter smells better than the ball?"

"I can believe it. That's one good-smelling man."

"Remind me to fire that agent."

"One of the other Bleeders has picked up the ball and is chewing on it. Looks like number eleven."

"Chewing. How original."

"Zaxter zips back up to the ceiling on his wire. He seems to have lured the injured player away from the ball so number eleven could pick it up. Good tactics."

"I'm just glad to see his harness— Dear God!"

"Ooh, looks like you spoke too soon, Jeff. That wire snapped like my prom date's g-string."

"What is wrong with you?"

"Good thing Zaxter is dressed like he's ready to disarm a bomb. Huh…who knew zombie teeth could rip through that?"

"To hell with this. I quit. Football is football? You people are sick."

"Wait Jeff, where are you— Well folks, after that bite, it looks like the Bleeders are going to have an extra player on the field and no handler. Will that be an advantage? We'll find out after this word from our sponsors."

Call Me Z

Like so many kids growing up in Ohio, where all forms of living dead were illegal, I grew up fascinated by zombies. The Saturday morning cartoon series *Dead Like Fred* had been my favorite from as early as I can remember. Eventually I graduated to zombie reality programs like *The Letter Z* and *Too Funny to Bury*. I dated girls obsessed with varying degrees of necrophilia, even losing my virginity to black-lipsticked Georgia Holloway in an open grave — her idea, not mine. So it surprised no one when, just hours after my high school graduation, I hopped in my rebuilt Datsun Z and headed for the Michigan border.

Michigan: the second state in the union to legalize domesticated zombies. The early adoption tripled Michigan's tourism industry and made Detroit the zombie capital of America. My best friend Joe-Joe had a friend with a place in the city I could crash with. Add to that eight hundred fifty-seven dollars in graduation gifts and it equals a guy ready to see some zombies.

See? No, I wasn't just looking to *see* zombies. I was out to immerse myself in zombie culture. I wanted to train a zombie as a house pet, exhibit one in a pageant, bet on zombie fights and races, film one falling off a trampoline and smashing its groin. Everything the stiffs on the nightly news called an indignity, a disgrace, a nightmare, that's what I wanted to be a part of. But more than anything, I wanted to stare a zombie in its bloodthirsty eye and kill it. Well, you know, kill it again.

I got hungry about the time I passed the Great Wall of Toledo, so I stopped in the town of Monroe for dinner. Not finding a single White Castle, I wound up at Denny's. On the door was a "No Zombies Allowed in Eating Establishments" decal that appeared government-issued. The decal's very existence suggested people here *tried* to bring zombies to dinner. Fascinating.

I asked for a booth by a window and ate my Grand Slam while I watched the street for more signs of zombies' integration to society. It was here I made my first sighting.

The sidewalk near this Denny's maintained a steady flow of foot traffic. Foot commuters, evening joggers, dog walkers. Then there was the woman in the short black skirt and three-inch heels. She was no supermodel, but the wriggle of her backside distracted me enough that I almost missed it. I probably would have missed the leash entirely if the man walking behind her hadn't borne the head of a snowman: carrot nose, top hat and all.

The snowman walked pretty well for a dead guy. Had he shambled or shuffled or limped, I would have noticed him immediately. The snowman's gait resembled Shaggy from Scooby Doo, a repetitive rolling step with stooped shoulders and a generally relaxed posture. It wasn't scary. Maybe the mask was a little creepy the way kids' birthday clowns were, but nothing like the hideous monsters on zombat.com.

The opaque snowman mask was attached to the leash in the shapely woman's hand. Just a woman out walking her snowman; nothing to see here. I knew people did it, but now I was actually watching someone walk her zombie. Honestly, it was a bit of a disappointment. No blood or guts? No *braaaiins*? I came looking for mindless beasts rejected from hell; what I got was a bobble-head on a leash.

I dropped a twenty on the table and chased after both snowman and skirt. I was disappointed, not dissuaded. I followed from a respectable distance, videoing them with my iphone. She noticed and waved with her fingers. I took it as an invitation to ask her about her zombie.

She was polite but not enthusiastic about the topic. She demonstrated how to lock and unlock the snowman helmet with a special key at the base of the neck — even let me unlock it and lock it back — but she stopped short of removing the apparatus; that process required the pet's limbs be secured lest it maul its keeper.

She even tolerated a partial interrogation. As it turns out her zombie is only a companion and she does not race, fight, show, or gamble with it. It is the only one she owns. A few but by no means all of her friends have their own zombies. It does not sleep per se but it stays locked in a special room while she sleeps. It wasn't until I asked if she had ever witnessed a live zombie attack that she remembered an urgent appointment for which she was already late and scampered off. I followed for three more blocks before she threatened to call the cops.

I passed a half dozen more zombies on the way back to Denny's, all out for evening strolls with their keepers. All wore some form of domestication headgear, mostly of the costume variety: a dog, a smiley face, Hello Kitty, a Lions' helmet, President Nixon. Not a scary figure in the bunch. Each one I passed made me want to squee like a girl at a boy-band concert. I was still two blocks from my car when I broke down and called Joe-Joe. He had the whole story by the time I started the engine.

"So Z finally got to see his zombie," Joe-Joe said. All my friends called me Z, after the star of the show *The Letter Z*. That guy was an ex-special forces soldier who demonstrated survival techniques in zombie-rich environments. It reportedly started as a legitimate instructional program, but Z was so over-the-top and sharp-witted that it became its own phenomenon. It was no stretch to say I wanted to be Z. Anything was better than being a guy named Eugene.

"But a snowman?" Joe-Joe continued. "Why the hell she dress him like a snowman in June?"

Poor little Joe-Joe, still so ignorant in the ways of zombie culture. "It's a deprivation helmet," I said. "So the zombie can't see or hear or smell. Take away a zombie's senses and it's as docile as a labradoodle."

"I thought deprivation helmets were like buckets you put on their heads."

"The original KarlCo ones still are, but other makers have turned them into fashion accessories. Paris Hilton's is diamond encrusted."

"She does make a hot zombie, doesn't she?" Joe-Joe was one of *those* zombie lovers: the literal kind.

"You're a sick puppy."

He barked into the phone.

"Dude, I'll send you the video. But I gotta go. Nez is expecting me at the Central Train Depot in Detroit in an hour and I'm not sure he'll wait." Nez was the guy I was crashing with. He had dated Joe-Joe's older sister for a couple years and had been kind of a big brother to Joe-Joe. I'd never met the guy myself.

I reached Detroit and got to the Central Depot a little early. The parking lot was vacant; no trains had run through here in years and the city never succeeded in repurposing the landmark. Now the building, the grounds, and the parking lot all looked like hell. Tumbleweeds of trash skittered around the pavement and caught against the curiously well-maintained fences. The Depot was its own little ghost town in the middle of Detroit.

The time of the rendezvous came and went. No Nez. I called his number and went straight to voicemail. He didn't even answer when I had Joe-Joe call.

I started the car and put the heat on to combat the growing chill of the night, as much psychological as meteorological. Maybe Nez had car trouble? I knew better. I'd been stood up. My grand trek to Detroit wasn't turning out so grand after all.

The sky turned a deep gray twilight while I used Google Maps to hunt down hotel accommodations. Paying for a room would cut this trip way short. Damn.

I was waiting for the driving directions to load to my phone when a vehicle pulled into the lot, the first since my Datsun. A shiny four-wheel-drive truck jacked up on huge tires. A wannabe monster truck. It rumbled over curbs and sidewalks and headed straight toward me. The floodlights atop the roll cage blinded me. It picked up speed as it closed in. Could this be Nez? Joe-Joe said the guy drove a Prius.

About the time I decided this behemoth was going to crush my car, the massive tires banked left and spun a donut through some empty parking spaces. It stopped with its lights aimed straight at me. The door opened and the driver hopped down.

Oh shit, he had a shotgun!

I thought about putting the car in gear and running for it, but either of those double barrels could have shattered my windshield and peppered me before I so much as laid a skidmark. A skidmark on the pavement, anyway. Instead I shut the engine off and killed the headlights, my wild kingdom submissive posture. Maybe I'd get lucky and he would just rob and not kill me. There was a Benjamin in my sock that could get me home. As long as he didn't strip-search me.

"Out of the car!" the shotgun man yelled.

I opened the door and climbed out, hands in the air. The last hints of daylight were gone and my captor stood in stark silhouette against the lights of his truck.

"Name," the shadow shouted.

"What?"

"Tell me your name, moth fucker, or I will repaint your car in red splat."
Did he call me a moth fucker?

"Name!" I heard the telltale sound of a shotgun being pumped. That's right, he pumped a double-barrel. That meant it was a custom built 1740, a showoff weapon favored by zombie hunters in Miami and New Orleans. It was a sweet gun. It was an expensive gun. It was not a gun I relished the idea of being shot with.

"Eugene!" I shouted a beat later than was probably wise. "My name is Eugene." Then quieter, "My friends call me Z."

"Z?" The shadow advanced. "Please say that's for your car."

I looked at the Datsun Z, on some level pleased he recognized the model. "Yeah, that," I said, "and for…"

"Shit." He rested the gun on his shoulder in a cool Clint Eastwood way. "Another zedhead."

Zedhead was what fans of *The Letter Z* called ourselves. "Yeah, guess I'm a Zedhead." So said the club membership card in my wallet. "You too?"

He turned and walked back toward his truck.

"Wait." I actually ran a few steps toward the man who had pointed a gun at my head. "Maybe you can help me. I was supposed to meet someone here."

He turned back around and held the gun in both hands, not pointed at me but still intimidating. "In the empty parking lot of an abandoned train station? In Detroit?"

"Yeah."

"Have you ever even seen a zombie, kid? Not on television, a real one."

"Of course I have." I didn't tell him how many or how recently I'd seen my first.

"Let me guess, just bucketheads."

I didn't say anything, but I think my face betrayed the truth.

He walked toward me and I could make out the five o'clock shadow and cleft chin against the glare behind him. Close enough I could smell the fries and overdone meat smell that permeated his flannel shirt. "Listen kid, I don't know how to tell you this, but someone's trying to get you killed."

"Killed?" I laughed. "Yeah, right." It was a nervous laugh, but still a laugh.

"Do you know what Central Depot is? This is the drop spot for zombies. Got a pet you don't want anymore? Bring it to Central. A friend that just turned? Bring him to Central. Got an annoying zombi-phile you want to give a wake-up call?"

"Send him to Central?"

"Sorry kid," the shadow said. "Look, zombies aren't toys. People get hurt. People die. Worse, people turn. So go back home and play with yourself while you still give a crap that you have a ding-dong."

Go home and play with yourself? I'd heard that line before, that voice before. "You're…you're Karl Yeager." The recognition chased all memories of the gun from my head. "Like, you're Mr. Zombie. You invented the deprivation helmet. And zombie biteguards. You hosted the first season of *Too Funny to Bury*. You—you're my fucking hero."

Yeager rolled his eyes and stepped out of the light beam. "Great. Yeah kid, I'm me. Now if you don't mind, I'm on the clock."

"On the clock? Are you hunting zombies? Holy crap, I get to watch Karl Yeager hunt zombies!"

"You get to haul your ass back home to Ohio where you came from."

It was that obvious? Ohio could cling to you like a stench. "Or you could let me off a zombie! Like on *Total Re-Kill*."

"Zombie killer? That what you think I am?"

The guy once hosted a home video program where zombies did hilarious things that often led to loss of limbs, and now he's at Detroit's zombie-pound with a 1740. What other conclusions could be reached?

Yeager seemed to be tracing the evidence himself and nodded slowly. "Fine. You want to see zombies? I have two here in the back." He walked to the rear of his truck. I followed a few paces behind, not sure if he was serious or kidding. Yeager patted a step below the bumper like he was summoning a dog to jump up. "Have a peek, zombie killer. They're ferocious."

Did he really have zombies in there? Animated or full corpses? Wild? Domesticated? I climbed the step and looked for myself.

There were indeed two zombies — a male and female — still animated but hogtied and wearing deprivation helmets, classic bucket-style. KarlCo helmets for sure. What else would Karl Yeager use? The two were rocking back and forth and I could hear them moaning even over the idling of the truck's oversized diesel.

"This one turned six months back," Yeager said, pointing to the male. "He was a pet. Her pet. She got bit today. Seems the locking mechanism on his helmet wasn't secured properly and he pulled out of it." He mumbled some profanity I couldn't quite decipher. "I got a call from a friend in Monroe, said these two were rampaging in the park."

Oh no. "The helmet he pulled out of, it was a snowman, wasn't it."

Yeager cocked his head. "Now how could you know that?"

It was the skirt. Tight and black, though the wriggle was suddenly far less appealing. "I saw them a few hours ago. She was taking him for a walk. I have video on my phone. I—" I couldn't bear to confess the rest.

"Huh." Yeager dropped the tailgate and climbed into the bed. He produced a pocket knife and cut the ropes. The zombies just lay there. They didn't flail or writhe or attack, just let their limbs fall limp while they moaned.

"They're so still," I said.

"Help me haul them out so you don't hurt the truck." He grabbed the male's foot and tugged him toward the open tailgate.

I only hesitated a moment before grabbing the other leg. When the time came to grab his arm to lower him to the ground, I was more reluctant. What if he grabbed me? Yeager seemed comfortable enough and their teeth were still inside their bucket-helmets, so I sucked it up and did my part. We set him on his feet and he remained standing. Then came the female. Joe-Joe would be disappointed that my hands didn't wander as we hefted her down. Her balance proved inferior and we had to lay her on the ground.

"Here's your chance." Yeager handed me the 1740. "You can leave the buckets on if you pay for them. Forty-nine ninety-nine apiece. I'll spare you the tax. Or I can take the helmets off, get a little adrenaline in you before you blow their faces open."

"Wait, what?" That gun was insanely heavy. "I thought you didn't kill zombies."

"I thought you did. Show me how it's done. I can video it so you can watch yourself on YouTube, if you like."

I admit, this wasn't how I envisioned zombie hunting. This was shooting fish in a barrel. Or in a bucket. No sport, no thrill. It felt like…well, murder.

I studied the zombies, I guess trying to find something about them that made it okay to shoot them. What I found was a gold band on the woman's left hand. The man's finger bore its match. They had been married. She had kept her zombie husband as a pet, a decision that eventually brought her here. Now they were together again. Did they know? Could zombies be happy?

"Too tame for you, killer? Here, let me get those off."

Yeager's words didn't even register until he had the helmets unlocked. If I remembered the Popular Mechanics issue correctly, unlocking the helm released the jaw, let air reach the nostrils, and of course allowed the helmet to be removed. I climbed into the truck bed and aimed the 1740. I wasn't ready to shoot them, but I wasn't opposed to defending myself if they charged.

Yeager pushed the male to the ground with minimal effort and pulled both helmets off at once. He threw the helmets into the bed beside me and followed them in. Even Karl Yeager wasn't taking these unbridled zombies lightly.

The zombie couple pushed unsteadily to their feet. She was just as attractive undead as alive save for the chunk missing from her cheek where you could see straight through to her molars. It must have been where hubby bit her. The wound was still wet, a sign I recognized as a mark of the recency of her change. Her hair was bedraggled but not knotted. Fingernails were already cached in dirt. Still, she was the same woman that had wriggled past the Denny's window only hours ago. She could have been, anyway. A survivable car crash could have done a lot more cosmetic damage.

Her spouse, on the other hand, was every bit of what I expected a zombie to be. His flesh was pale green and cached with dry pus where bacteria had settled unchallenged. He had small wounds all over, each dry and dusty. He had been sufficiently kempt that there were no noticeable pockets of maggots or worms, but chunks of his face had been rubbed clear through to the bone, probably when he pulled free of the helmet. What hair remained on his head formed a web of gnarls no comb could ever penetrate. Only one of his eyes was open and it was noticeably clouded, even in the dim light provided by the truck's cargo lamp.

The zombies seemed to consider each other a moment before their noses recognized the true prizes in the area. They lumbered toward the truck. Damn, they were slow. "How can anyone be afraid of one of these?" It was a genuine question.

"Don't let them fool you, they're wicked strong," Yeager assured me. "And they don't stop getting up. You want to be scared? Go inside the depot. Dozens in there, maybe hundreds.

"So go on, kill them," Yeager taunted. "You can owe me on the ammunition."

I handed the gun back to him, barrels to the sky, hand nowhere near the trigger. "You know I'm not going to."

"I'm not here to stop you, kid. They're nothing to me."

"Enough, all right. I just…never thought of them as people before."

"Some say they aren't. They were, sure, but those people died. What's driving those bodies now is something else. Can't say what, but they ain't human."

I shook my head.

"So now what, Z?" Yeager said.

The two zombies had reached the truck. The woman slapped the fenders with her hands. The man was using his face similarly. Pitiful, dumb creatures. Once I might have even laughed at them, too stupid to even climb.

"Not Z," I said. "Just call me Eugene."

ABOUT THE AUTHOR

Scott W. Baker has been writing science fiction and fantasy since 1999, though by day he teaches math to high school students. In 2010, his story "Poison Inside the Walls" placed in the prestigious Writers of the Future competition. He lives in Tennessee with his wife and daughter.

Visit his website at http://scottwbaker.net